# G R JORDAN

# Winter Slay Bells

*A Highlands and Islands Detective Thriller*

First edition

ISBN: 978-1-915562-60-9

This book was professionally typeset on Reedsy.
Find out more at reedsy.com

Far off down the road, through the lazily drifting snowflakes, they could hear the merry sound of sleigh bells. Their gay little tinkling flying ahead of the sleigh and lighting up the night with sparks.

BETTY MACDONALD

# Contents

# Foreword

The events of this book, while based around real locations around Inverness, are entirely fictional and all characters do not represent any living or deceased person. All companies are fictitious representations. It's a Christmas blether!

# Acknowledgement

To Ken, Jean, Colin, Evelyn, John and Rosemary for your work in bringing this novel to completion, your time and effort is deeply appreciated.

# Books by G R Jordan

The Highlands and Islands Detective series (Crime)

1. Water's Edge
2. The Bothy
3. The Horror Weekend
4. The Small Ferry
5. Dead at Third Man
6. The Pirate Club
7. A Personal Agenda
8. A Just Punishment
9. The Numerous Deaths of Santa Claus
10. Our Gated Community
11. The Satchel
12. Culhwch Alpha
13. Fair Market Value
14. The Coach Bomber
15. The Culling at Singing Sands
16. Where Justice Fails
17. The Cortado Club
18. Cleared to Die
19. Man Overboard!
20. Antisocial Behaviour
21. Rogues' Gallery
22. The Death of Macleod - Inferno Book 1

Kirsten Stewart Thrillers (Thriller)

Jac Moonshine Thrillers

1. Jac's Revenge
2. Jac for the People
3. Jac the Pariah


Siobhan Duffy Mysteries

1. A Giant Killing
2. Death of the Witch
3. The Bloodied Hands


The Contessa Munroe Mysteries (Cozy Mystery)

1. Corpse Reviver
2. Frostbite
3. Cobra's Fang


The Patrick Smythe Series (Crime)

1. The Disappearance of Russell Hadleigh
2. The Graves of Calgary Bay
3. The Fairy Pools Gathering

Austerley & Kirkgordon Series (Fantasy)

1. Crescendo!
2. The Darkness at Dillingham
3. Dagon's Revenge
4. Ship of Doom

Supernatural and Elder Threat Assessment Agency (SETAA) Series (Fantasy)

1. Scarlett O'Meara: Beastmaster

Island Adventures Series (Cosy Fantasy Adventure)

1. Surface Tensions

Dark Wen Series (Horror Fantasy)

1. The Blasphemous Welcome
2. The Demon's Chalice

# Chapter 01

Alice Greenwood stood up from her coffee, lifted the shopping bags beside her, and strode out of the café. She needed to crack on. After all, this was her day off. She'd had to fudge it, had to make sure that she got it so she could get ready for Christmas. It would not be that long before the day was here, and she had plenty to do. Inverness was busy with shoppers looking to grab presents before the big day. Before you knew it, Christmas Eve would be on your doorstep.

The shop where she worked was already busy. Best described as a discount art shop with a selection of books and other materials, The Biz sold remaindered stock. Alice's team was stretched thin by the demise of Muriel and the abrupt leaving of Patricia a month ago. They'd advertised, but those who had applied were not suitable. Alice wanted to make sure she got someone in who could do the job properly, not a fly-by-night.

It left her short on the team for Christmas and a few of them had asked for time off for parties and Christmas events with the kids, but she hadn't time to give. Alice had to get her day in, first and foremost, and that was today. Hence, she was running around like an insane fly trapped inside a car windscreen.

Christmas Eve was going to be special this year, though. There was a golf club dance. John would be there. He didn't know it yet, but she was going to knock him over. Otherwise, it was going to be Christmas alone, and she wasn't having that. He could spend it with her. After all, he was on his own too after the divorce. He'd clearly been interested and, with an outfit she was going to buy, she'd make sure he was interested. After all, what else would he be doing this Christmas?

She needed to stop running herself down like that. She wasn't the only option, but she was the one he would want, the one he would choose.

Alice wished she hadn't chosen to wear her high heels, but she wanted them on so she could try the dress. It all would have to look perfect together, but right now, she wished she'd taken a pair of trainers and thrown the shoes in the bag with her. She stopped, reached down, and ran her finger inside the strap at the back of her ankle. As she did so, somebody caught her on the shoulder.

'Hey, careful,' she said. A young lad looked down, throwing an apology at her as he ran off.

'Flipping kids,' she said. She was never having any. She looked across to her left and saw what she thought was the folly of Christmas. Everything was over-hyped. She couldn't believe this year Inverness was going to have its own Christmas Eve shindig. Santa Claus was coming, and they'd built a stage with a large backdrop of a house, at the top of which was a massive chimney. Santa was going to appear complete with the sack on his back. Alice shook her head; she wouldn't be here. She'd be making sure that John knew where to spend Christmas. The stage was such a waste of money, though.

'The big stage' had been the talk of the town ever since it was first announced back in October. There would be special guests coming until the big man himself arrived. The town was in a frenzy. The council had done wonders this year. Shoppers were pouring in, and she had felt it in the shop. Their takings were way up, but the workload was immense. Maybe the economic crisis from earlier on in the year had caused everyone to decide to sod it this Christmas. 'Let's just blow whatever money we have.'

The punters were certainly out and about, and Alice looked down at the bags she had with her. Admittedly, a lot of hers weren't Christmas presents. Most of her money had been spent on herself. And most of it had been spent to impress John—the new underwear, especially. And then she got the cookbook and started buying ingredients. *He's getting me plus food. He won't resist, will he?*

And those special earrings she bought, plus the perfume. The price tag was rising fast. But she had to go all-out to capture a man, and now was the time to do it—now when he was on the rebound. Now when he was shell-shocked by the divorce. His wife had dumped it on him, and it was the one thing that Alice wondered about. Still, if there was something so bad about him, she could always let him go after a month. She would not spend Christmas alone.

Taking one last look back at the large stage with the ridiculously sized chimney, Alice marched along the high street towards the shopping centre. Inside was just as busy and she strode off towards the department store. She was looking for a bit of class, but she wasn't daft. Alice wasn't a young girl. She'd dress provocatively. She'd make sure that he knew he was getting a fine lady. But she would not look like some of the older women did. Mutton dressed as a lamb, her mother had called it. *Am I trying too hard?*

Alice pressed the screen of her phone, activating the audiobook that spoke to her through the pods in her ears. *Beating Insecurity* it was called. There was a woman droning on about how insecurity was fear. Fear of what you weren't, telling Alice to be positive. To remind herself of all the things that she had. Why was she so worthwhile to others?

As she entered the clothing section of the department store, she wondered if she was worthwhile to others. After all, she was trying to seduce a man for Christmas Eve. A man with clearly nothing else to do. Looking for him to come home with her, bed her, and then feed him the next day. Was that just being desperate?

She had a friend who didn't understand this need for a man. And Alice, in truth, didn't understand her friend. No one to hold her at night, no one to wake up with, no one to eat with. Her friend would come out for coffee, might even appear for the odd meal together, but there wasn't anybody in her life except her cat.

Alice hated the cat. It would come and rub itself up against her legs. She wanted a man. She wanted somebody to hold her, somebody to make her feel good, to tell her she was beautiful. *Was that insecurity?*

*Screw this*, thought Alice, and took the pods out of her ears and switched off the audiobook. *This is what I'm doing, and this is how I'm doing it. I need to stop listening to these books. They just screw with your head.*

She stepped forward and started looking around some racks of clothing, and decided they looked rather matronly. She moved along to the clothes for a slightly younger age, not for the overly mature woman. Alice picked one outfit out and stood in front of the mirror looking at it.

*Well, I'd have a heck of a cleavage showing*, she thought. *That could be good.*

There was, however, a large slit up the side of the dress. Alice wasn't very impressed with her thighs. There was too much cellulite. She didn't want to look like she was trying to be something she wasn't. She was no model figure, but the boys like something extra to hold at night, don't they? That's what the songs say, don't they? Well, didn't they?

She turned round and put the dress back on the rack, then lifted it off again, then put it back. She moved along to a little red number, picked it up, and picked up a green one. Then she went back to the blue one she'd picked up once already and marched off with the three of them towards the changing rooms. As she entered the extensive area behind the main shop where the changing rooms were, she saw a young girl manning the station.

'How many items?' she asked politely.

Alice held up the three of them. 'Three, please.'

She was handed a number three on a large white piece of card. As she took it, she thought she saw the girl glance down at the dresses and then up at her. Was she sniggering? Was she having a laugh? Alice didn't entertain her. Instead, she marched on, examining the changing cubicles.

There was a man in that changing room. You could tell for he was changing his top with the curtain open. His wife was standing behind him. *Look at the jumper*, she thought. That's what she didn't want, somebody boring like that. John wasn't boring. He liked a bit of a gamble. He also had that sports car.

She continued walking until she got halfway down and

selected a changing room that was away from everyone else.

Alice hung up the three dresses and stood for a moment, looking at them. *The blue one*, she thought. *If I can get in that blue one, he's not going to take his eyes off me. It certainly shows a lot*, she thought. Could she carry it off?

Alice took off the jeans she was wearing, pulled off her jumper and her t-shirt and stood in her underwear. Her bra was a rather drab and supportive affair, the kind you wear because it's comfortable. After all, nobody else was going to see it. She pulled on the blue dress over the top and stood and looked at herself in the mirror.

*I can get away with the legs*, she thought. The slit wasn't as high as she'd reckoned, and her thighs were probably contained underneath it. She looked at her cleavage. The bra was showing. 'Certainly, plenty of cleavage,' she thought, and for a moment, was proud of herself. Proud of the way she looked. You were born with what you got, but you had to use what you were given. That's what her mum always told her. Alice laughed, remembering it.

She pulled off the blue dress and hung it back up. She went to try on the red and the green one, but no. No, the blue one was the one she wanted. Would the other underwear work with it, though? Maybe she'd need a bigger size. She could get the size up in the blue dress. See if that fitted better, maybe it would adjust better. She didn't want her underwear on show, after all. She didn't want to look tarty.

She pulled back the curtain slightly, making sure it was wrapped around her as she stood in her underwear, and shouted out for the assistant. The young girl seemed to have disappeared, but Alice noticed that there was somebody beside her. The next changing room had the curtain pulled across, though the man and his wife from further up had disappeared.

*Stuff it*, she thought, closing the curtain. She undid her bra, throwing it on the floor and whipped off her bottoms. Alice rummaged in her bag, pulled out the new underwear she'd bought and put it on. She stood looking at herself for a moment. *Well, if he doesn't get excited by this, the man is dead and not worth it,* she thought to herself.

There was background music playing in the changing rooms. The usual Christmas fare. Something struck Alice. She was used to hearing sleigh bells when something like 'Winter Sleigh Ride' came on, or 'Troika'. That jingling sound, constantly being rung back and forward as the music bounced along, but this wasn't that. The music being played was a rock and roll number. And yes, it was singing about Christmas, but she could remember no sleigh bells. The sleigh bells were ringing, gently at first before growing in volume.

*Not to worry,* she thought. *Whatever that nonsense is.* She grabbed the blue dress, pulled it on over her underwear, and adjusted it before looking in the mirror.

Damn, that was good. She leant forward slightly. It was very full-on. Very! He certainly couldn't miss her.

Alice turned around, looking over her shoulder in the mirror. No, her bum didn't look big in it. It actually looked quite good. She turned back again, pulling the dress this way and that. She wouldn't need a bigger size. This was daring, truly daring.

It was those sleigh bells again. They were louder now. Ringing away. They weren't in time, though, not with the song. There was no rhythm to it. Just constant. They weren't part of the music. They were here in the now. She turned and pulled back the curtain and looked out. They were here all right. She stepped out of the changing room. *What on earth?*

*Was she just not getting it?* It must have been on the sound system. Beside her, the changing room was empty. She looked up and down, but there was no one in.

Alice turned back and stood looking in the mirror for a moment. She'd forgotten to close the curtain behind her, and as she looked, she could see right through to the changing room behind. There was no one there.

She reached down, picked her brush out of her handbag, and did her hair. She let it come down one side, seeing if she could let it straggle down past her neck, reaching down towards her chest. Alice looked down, brushing it. And then, when she looked up, someone was over her shoulder.

A white-gloved hand reached up to her shoulder, and she saw a blade above her, which was driven down and into her. Pain raced through her shoulder, and she collapsed, twisting awkwardly on the floor. As she turned round, she looked up to see a masked assailant—an assailant dressed in a red hat, a Christmas one like Santa would wear. There was a mask on, with the happy, gleeful face of an elf. The figure was not much bigger than she, but it was dressed in a green suit with red trim, white here and there. A Christmas Elf. The elf on the shelf. Now the elf with a butcher's knife.

Alice put her hands up, but the ferocity of the attack overwhelmed her. The knife was plunged down time and time again. Alice's body racked with pain. The adrenaline kept her fighting momentarily, helped her to stay alive long enough to see the blows repeat. The white-gloved elf brought the large knife to bear on her time and again. Its gloves turned red, the mask covered in blood.

As the life seeped away from Alice, she saw the elf step out of the changing room, close the curtain, and there again came the sound of sleigh bells. Slowly, they died away. The sound gradually reduced in intensity, almost matching Alice's heart as it slowed its beats and eventually stopped.

# Chapter 02

Seoras Macleod was in what he would call a reasonably good place. Not where he was physically standing, but mentally. He'd come back to the job, albeit with someone extra. The recent cases had taken their toll on him, and his mind had suffered to such a point that he now saw a figure next to him. It would come and go. Sometimes it was across the room, sometimes it was next to him, whispering something in his ear. It was in a grey monk's habit and although he never quite saw the face, he knew it was the man who had attacked him. The man who had set him up to be beaten; the man who had looked to kill him. A man who was now under the waters of Stornoway Harbour.

Macleod had almost accepted the fact that the figure would show up. Occasionally he even spoke to it, though he did hope that it would go away. In most of daily life, he could get by with it being there, but he knew Jane was finding it awkward. It was hard to be intimate when you thought there was somebody watching.

For this and other reasons, he was delighted to be out on this evening, sipping an apple juice, watching his staff enjoy themselves. They had hired a room and devoured a large buffet.

Now at the far end, in front of a karaoke machine, Clarissa Urquhart was belting out a tune that Macleod wasn't sure was ever sung quite in that fashion. She had her arm around Patterson, and the poor lad was looking like he didn't want to be there.

Clarissa had developed a fondness for him because she'd saved Patterson's life after he'd taken a knife to the throat; it was one of many occurrences that had driven Clarissa to decide that she would leave the murder squad. Macleod couldn't blame her. He probably never should have brought her on to the team. She wasn't cut out for some sights she saw, but she was such a tough nut. He had needed her then. He didn't anymore. Hope had matured into an excellent detective inspector. She had Susan Cunningham behind her, and there was Ross.

Macleod picked up a sausage roll and bit into it and then saw his detective inspector making her way towards him. Hope was the on-call from the team that night, and had dressed in her jeans, t-shirt, and leather jacket. Partners were allowed with them, but John had decided not to come. Hope slid her way over to Macleod, an orange juice in hand.

'She had much to drink?'

'More than me,' said Macleod. 'I don't think she needs the drink. I think she's more than capable of . . . whatever that is, sober.'

Hope looked around her and smiled. 'We've needed this, haven't we? We've needed a break. The last week or two's been quiet, giving everybody a time to relax. It's good to see Clarissa before she goes as well.'

'I'm delighted she's taking the opportunity and not leaving the force.'

'Art thefts, specialist role. I think you had something to do with that,' said Hope.

'I owed her,' said Macleod, 'but I've paid for it.'

'Paid for it? In what way?'

'Well, I'm the supervising officer. She'll be running the investigations. She'll be moving up to detective inspector, but I'll be the Chief Inspector over the top. That's the trouble when you move up, your portfolio opens up. I'm not sure I'm happy with it.'

'You'd rather be back down where I am, would you?'

'You know I would,' said Macleod.

'There are rumours she's going to take somebody with her. I'm worried it's going to be Ross.'

'Why worried? He's entitled to move on. He's entitled to find his own way, and you'll find someone else. Susan's doing well.'

'Susan's very green still,' said Hope. 'Ross has got his own talents. Susan's more like me.'

'Then you go and you find someone with those talents. You diversify. You bring people on. It's not a one-stop shop.'

'I know that. Patterson's not Ross though.'

'Nobody's Ross,' said Macleod. 'Nobody's you. Nobody's me. It's all a mix. It's all a dynamic. Put it all together and see what comes out the other end.'

'It's good of you giving Clarissa that time off before she starts as well.'

'Well, she never got a proper honeymoon, did she? With everything that went on, her storming back in, she could do with some time off with her man. Christmas is a good time. Although she's doing the art thefts, she could be required to travel all over the country. It's a side to her we never fully

12

made use of.'

'Well, we didn't have that many art thefts involved with murders. We can't stipulate that someone's going to nick something arty each time they kill someone.'

'That would be a better reason than most of them have,' said Macleod.

'Do you think she'll take Ross?'

Macleod looked over and saw his partner Jane, dancing alongside Ross's partner, Angus. The pair had become firm friends after Angus had taken her in during one case when Jane's life had looked under threat.

'I'm not so sure you'll have to worry about that.'

'Has she told you something?' said Hope. 'Don't you hold out on me. I'm your DI now. You need to tell me these things. After all, it's my team you're talking about.'

'She's told me nothing. She's requested nothing. Although she needs to do it soon.'

'So, what's with all the coy comments?' said Hope.

She had turned now, looking down at Macleod, those several inches she had on him being made to bear. Hope was always an imposing figure, red of hair, six feet tall, and in great shape. She could intimidate most men. Intimidate and excite. But Macleod just smiled. It had taken time, but the two of them had struck up a proper friendship.

'I just think I know how she works.'

'She charges in like a bull in a China shop.'

'No,' said Macleod. 'When you first started, I didn't know how you worked. I didn't see someone with certain insecurities. You still have them, but you know how to deal with them now. Instead, I saw a six-foot-tall redhead with incredible confidence, ready to take on the world.'

13

'You saw a tart,' said Hope, laughing. 'You saw someone you thought was a jezebel.'

'That's a word you've learnt from me,' said Macleod. 'I wasn't in a good place then. I'm in a better place now,' he said, nodding at Jane. 'The thing about Clarissa is, everyone sees the bull in the China shop. Everyone sees the woman that kicks up a storm, the woman who takes a battering and then comes through. Few see the softer side.'

'Well, she's not soft around women as far as I understand it,' said Hope, 'so no, I haven't.'

'Frank's seen it,' said Macleod. 'Look at her at the moment.'

'Yes,' said Hope, 'raising hell.'

'With her arm around a person who nearly died. With her arm around a person who struggles to fit into this team at the moment. She cares more than you ever know, more than I ever know. She's just got a rather brutal way of showing it.'

'So, what, she's going to take Ross out of her generous, caring attitude, rather than just picking the best for her team?'

Macleod laughed. A man in a hood standing beside him said, 'She just doesn't get it. She doesn't get it. Maybe she's not ready for this. You're leaving the team in a bad way, Seoras.'

'No, I'm not,' said Macleod under his breath.

'What did you say?' asked Hope. The music was loud, and she wasn't sure what Macleod had said.

'I'm just talking to the man beside me.'

'Will that never go away?' asked Hope.

'Well, I asked the doctors, and they don't know. I asked the man himself and he doesn't know, so I don't know.'

'I'm here to stay. You're never getting rid of me.'

Macleod watched as the imaginary man took to the middle of the dance floor as Jane gyrated this way and that in a rather haphazard fashion. The man in the monk's outfit stood beside her. The face was always in shadow, always unseen, but the hood looked straight at Jane. However, it attacked no one. It never even reached for them. The doctors said this is because Macleod's mind knew it couldn't, knew it couldn't interact with anyone else around him. It could only interact with him because he let it.

*Let it. What a word, what a way to put it*, Macleod had thought. *Even if I'd had, he could have at least coaxed me round to the idea I could deal with it.*

'I hope you get past it,' said Hope. 'Not something good to live your life with.'

'It's not, and keep this to yourself,' said Macleod. 'I'm only saying this because it's you,' Hope raised her eyebrows. 'When you're trying to be closer, a little more intimate, a man in a monk's outfit doesn't really help.'

'Are you two struggling on that side?'

'She's been brilliant,' said Macleod. 'Incredibly understanding, but it's not made it easy.'

For a moment the two of them stood looking out into the middle of the room and then Hope sipped on her drink. 'Thanks for sharing that with me,' she said. 'I'm sure the next time me and John are intimate, I won't be checking around the room to make sure nobody's there.'

Macleod laughed, but then his face took on a slight weariness.

'Anyway, have you seen the shenanigans in the middle of town?' he asked.

'Do you mean the big stage? There's a massive Christmas do being put on and there's going to be quite a few stars.'

'Local radio people, Hope. I mean, it's not as if anybody big

15

from the music industry's coming, is it?'

'There's some decent local stuff.'

'Nobody I recognise,' said Macleod.

'You're not into music,' said Hope. 'Stop getting down on it. It's good for the town. Place is buzzing. Let it buzz. Life's good, Seoras. We've had a rough time. Time to chill. It's time to . . .'

Hope reached into her pocket, feeling the vibration of her pager. She looked at Macleod briefly and disappeared out of the room, returning a minute later. She waved Cunningham over to her before making her way over to Macleod.

'Did you speak too soon?' he said.

'Way too soon. Got a body in one of the department stores.'

'Are they sure it's a murder?'

'There's blood everywhere, and it looks like they've been hacked to death. They don't know who did it, but they sure as heck know it was a murder.'

'You best get on. I see Jona's on her way.'

The diminutive Asian woman had also been at the party, but being shy, she had quietly stood at the side. Now she'd slipped out. Macleod wondered if anybody had even noticed.

'Let me know when you have the details. I'll pop along if you need me.'

'I'll do my best to cope without anyone. Let them have their night. Looks like they might work over Christmas after all.'

Macleod nodded and let Hope turn away. As she strode to the door, he watched her closely. She was ready. She was the DI, and she was ready. Someone took him by the arm.

'Where's she gone?' asked Jane, his partner.

'Start of a case.'

Macleod turned and smiled at her. Jane was looking well

tonight, happy, but then Jane could always do the social occasions. She reached over and kissed him on the cheek, and then she tilted her head and kissed him on the lips. She did it three times. And then she remained holding his hand while she stepped back. 'Tell your hooded friend that's from me.'

Macleod pulled her close again, and she turned around. He held her as the two of them looked at the partying people before them. Up on the stage, Clarissa was still singing. Angus was dancing on the floor, and Ross was sipping away at a pint. There were plenty of others from the station. Macleod felt relaxed. With one arm, he hugged Jane and with the other, he raised his glass and gave a toast to the man in the far corner wearing the monk's habit. Jane reached behind her onto the table and picked up a glass of fizzy wine.

'Is he over there?'

'Yes,' said Macleod, 'he's over there.'

Jane raised her glass. 'Here's to you,' she said. 'May you rot in hell.'

She drank her wine and Macleod wasn't sure what he thought about what she said, but the man could certainly go away.

# Chapter 03

Hope McGrath rubbed her eyes with the back of her hand. It was now three in the morning and all she wanted was to be at home lying in bed with John's arms wrapped around her. She'd called him recently, following up on the text she'd sent almost as soon as she'd got the call to come to the department store. It had taken a while for Jona to go through her processes, but once she had done, Hope had visited the crime scene.

There was very little indication of who the attacker was, but there was blood everywhere. Jona said that was a good thing. They might trace blood splatter on the killer, but they'd have to find them first. One problem with the changing room was so many people had been in and out of it during the day. Finding someone's DNA there could be dismissed as a normal visit to the changing rooms.

The victim had fallen on the floor, knifed as she lay in there. The assistant for the changing room had been out. She'd gone off on her break. The young girl hadn't found the deceased woman. Instead, a customer had come in looking to try on clothes and had seen the red stains at the far end of the changing room. She got slightly closer then ran screaming.

They checked that witness, and it was clear that she hadn't carried out the killing. If she had, the clothing she was wearing would have been covered in blood. She'd also been seen throughout the store. There was a CCTV link that focused on the changing room, but it had gone down not long before. The CCTV on the doors was working, and they could certainly see who was about the store, but to what picture quality remained to be seen. Ross would go through the CCTV the next day. But with so many people about, and the camera that was pointed to the dressing room having been taken out of action, Hope wasn't sure that they would get much from it.

Hope spent a while with one of the local sergeants. The next morning, Uniform would do 'stop and ask' throughout the city centre, seeing if anyone had been in town the previous day. The death hadn't occurred late on in the day. Having cordoned off the scene, the Sergeant had decided it was clearly a murder and called in the team in the early evening.

'Are we fully covered?' Susan Cunningham asked Hope.

The two women stood inside the store, and Hope mentally ran through what she had to do for the next day.

'We've got Uniform prepped to go and talk to those who we can identify off CCTV. We've got all the store workers to go through. We've nearly finished off the initial questions with them. Most of them will be eliminated because they'll be on the footage.'

'Have we got a time of death?'

'Before two, because that's when the woman who found her walked in. The changing room went quiet for quite a while. The attendant who had been on earlier said it had been rather busy. She remembered Alice Greenwood going in carrying three dresses. She went off for lunch, came back, and obviously, things had deteriorated rapidly. However, she had said that it had been busy during the day. You can't conduct a killing like this if it's been busy.'

'We have got an ID; Alice Greenwood,' said Susan Cunningham. 'Apparently, she's the boss of a shop just down the road from here. She wasn't at work today, but one of the store workers recognised her.'

'All right, we best get there in the morning then.'

'The other thing is that Jona's come up with a card. Apparently, it was lying underneath the body, had been thrown there. Although Jona is not sure about how that happened, whether it was dropped at the time or whether it was done after, but it was lying underneath in an envelope.'

'Where is Jona? She needs to update me, anyway.'

'You speak my name and I appear. It is I, the Christmas fairy.'

'I think that's a bit dry for the moment, isn't it?' said Hope. She smiled as her friend appeared.

'I need to take a break,' said Jona. 'Come and join me out in the van. I'll get one of the team to make you some coffee as well. I'm sure you could do with it.'

Hope joined Jona, along with Susan Cunningham, a couple of minutes later in the back of the forensic wagon. Jona had taken off her suit and stood in jeans and a t-shirt, pointing up at some pictures that had been taped to the wall. 'The knife, it looks something like that,' said Jona. 'Wide blade, deep cuts. I don't think she'd have stood a chance. Looks like it was a frenzied attack. Lots of blood everywhere. Whoever it was would have been covered.'

'How did they get out then?' asked Hope.

'I think they've changed before leaving. Think about it. If you're going into a changing room, you can go in with bags, you can go in with the clothing you want to get changed into, come back out again, wrap everything up. If you wear gloves, you can then snap them off into a bag as well and disappear out.'

'It's a very high-risk murder,' said Hope.

'Very high-risk,' said Jona. 'She could have screamed. She could have called for someone. Alice Greenwood might have gone into shock and not been able to speak. The blade looks to maybe have come at her from behind. There's a cut, which would show that it stabbed Alice in the back. Given that she's on the floor now, I'm surmising she might have turned, but this is quite subjective. What did happen, was she was then on the floor and stabbed multiple times. She wouldn't have lasted long, not with the number of times she was knifed.'

'You found a card as well. Is that correct?' asked Hope.

'Yes,' said Jona, and pointed to a bag sitting at the side.

'We opened up the card. Inside it, it's got the inscription written in pen. *Listen. Hear them ringing. Embrace your festive doom.*'

'That's catchy,' said Susan. 'I don't recognise it, though.'

'Me neither,' said Hope. 'Embrace your festive doom. That doesn't sound like an ordinary killer. Also, hear them ringing. Hear what ringing?'

'I don't know that,' said Jona. 'All I can do is give you what's there, tell you what it says. We'll see if we can pick up any fingerprints or anything else off the card. We'll need to look at where it was bought too or if it's handmade. Looking at it, there are no marks on the back. It may be handmade, but we can look at where the materials come from as well. However, if they're basic, could be any number of places?'

'Just to clarify,' said Hope. 'Someone walks into the changing rooms of this department store, where there are shoppers everywhere going back and forward. They take out a large knife, stab a woman to death, causing plenty of blood and mayhem, and walk back out of here.'

'Is there any other way out?' asked Susan.

'I don't know,' said Jona. 'I've been concentrating mainly on the scene. You think there might be?'

'There might be a back way out, somewhere for the staff to head to their restroom or whatever? It's not uncommon. Stores don't work the same as houses, do they?' said Susan. 'It's very easy to have voids in the back, or to just put up a partition. You then have a corridor that's nothing more than glorified cardboard and concrete floor.'

'That's a good thought. Find out for me,' said Hope.

Susan disappeared, and Hope stood sipping her coffee.

'Clarissa's on the move,' said Jona, 'and I heard Macleod gave her all of Christmas off.'

'Yes, that's why I'm here. I got cover.'

'I always cover when it's a team day out, me and, of course, one other. He was here first, but given what it was, I thought I should come along and help him.'

'You're all heart, aren't you?' said Hope.

'I wish I wasn't. I truly wish I wasn't,' said Jona. 'Truth is, I don't have a lot to do this time of year.'

'What are you doing for Christmas?'

'I'm going to be here,' said Jona, 'Stuck here. I would have liked to go off to the folks, but I can't get the cover. When you're the boss, and especially with this now happening, you won't get time to get away. I was hoping I might have got time with mum and dad. That was the plan. Hopefully, this doesn't blow up into anything else.'

'You think it is something?'

'Initially, no. When I looked at it,' said Jona, 'you've had someone come in and knife someone in such a brutal fashion. These types of killings are usually ad hoc, opportunistic. What bothers me is the fact that they sailed in and out with nobody noticing.'

'Somebody who did it opportunistically wouldn't come prepared with clothing to change into. They'd be running out of here with blood dripping into busy Christmas streets. He'd be seen,' said Hope. 'You're right.'

'Then there's the card. We don't know what that card means, but "listen, hear them ringing", that shows a connection. That shows that they're talking about something. "Embrace your festive doom."'

'I'm not so sure,' said Hope. '"Embrace your festive doom" sounds so general. "Hear them ringing." Does that mean they know what they are or was there just something at the time?'

Hope finished her coffee and strode back into the store, where an excited Susan Cunningham ran up to her. 'There is a door in the back. There is a door out. It runs into the back of the store and comes out again. From it, you can get up to the restroom. You can go anywhere in the rear of that store. They could have appeared somewhere else.'

'Is that the way they came in, then?' asked Hope. 'Think about it. You could come in that way and hide until you knew that section was clear.'

'Are we thinking this is planned or are we thinking this is an opportunistic attack?'

'The way she's been murdered, the amount of force, the action with the knife,' said Hope, 'that's saying it's opportunistic. But not getting caught, not running out with blood in your

23

hands. I'd expect in a murder like this for us to be finding the culprit almost straight away. There'd be clues everywhere. There'd be bits and pieces of them left about. I'm not so sure, though.'

'If you planned it like that, why kill them in this way?'

'Rage?' said Hope.

'It doesn't look like rage, though. If you can get in and out, how does that work?'

'I don't know, Susan,' said Hope. 'I don't know. We've got someone who's clever enough to get in and out without being seen. They've caused a massive amount of blood to be spilt around the place. Yet, they've been clever enough to not be seen. They've cut off the CCTV. Why? So they can walk in, so they can walk out? Or as a diversion? Are they afraid things might go wrong? How much do they know? It's brazen. It's the middle of the day.'

'I'm wondering,' said Susan, 'if they got disturbed, were they just able to disappear, because they'd come through the back, to pretend they were staff? Did they turn anyone away? We need to do the trawl. We won't know enough until we've done the trawl.'

'She was discovered reasonably soon after.'

'People are in and out of these shops like anything. We'll put out the word and go on TV as well,' said Susan. 'We should do that. We should ask for any witnesses or anyone who was around at the time to come and give their statements. It's going to be a trawl. It's going to be tomorrow at the earliest that we can piece together what happened.'

Hope nodded. 'In the meantime,' she said, 'I'll get Jona to check that passage at the back. She'll need to go through it with a fine-tooth comb, see if anything's been dropped, if there's any evidence in there. Staff will go up and down there. If we find anything, or anyone who wasn't staff, we might have a chance of at least getting pointed in the right direction. Anything else?' Hope asked.

'No,' said Susan.

'Right, I'm going to collect my thoughts,' said Hope. 'A quick walk is needed. You stay here. Make sure Jona's aware of that rear passageway and get her to check it out for us. I'll need to be heading back to see Macleod. He'll be in early. It won't be like him to not want a briefing early on.'

Hope left the building and took a walk into the town. There was the occasional street cleaner up, but otherwise, the place was deserted, and ever so quiet. A very occasional car rolled through. The Christmas lights were off. The centre of the city had the road blocked off.

Hope looked over at the large stage in the centre of Inverness. There were posters everywhere about the festive season and shopping. The Christmas season would be good for the city, fantastic. They'd have to be careful about how they asked for information. They didn't want to spook people. A random, vicious knife attack in the middle of the department store.

Hope looked up at the stage with its housing backdrop behind it and the large chimney that Santa would come and visit in less than a week's time.

*Wrong time for a murder*, she thought. *The provost isn't going to be happy about this. We need to solve this quickly. Otherwise, the town's going to take a hit. Who wants to come and go shopping when there's a killer on the loose?*

# Chapter 04

'You could have taken a few hours,' said Hope.

She walked into Macleod's office, trying to give a smile and appear bright and breezy. But she was exhausted. She'd worked through the night and got to that point where really, she wanted to go to bed. You felt like your very bones were sore on the inside and everything just became that little harder to focus on. You didn't become a blubbering idiot; it's just you weren't sharp. Appearing before Seoras and not being sharp often felt like you were leaving yourself open. He was always sharp, always quick to the whatever point was being made.

'Well, I'm not long in,' he said.

'You are. Secretary said you've been in here since five. You've already had a few people up who were going off shift to run you through the basics. I was coming in to tell you, as always.'

'I know, but I just like things from different points of view, different angles. Sometimes, there's . . .'

'What?' asked Hope. 'Things I might have missed.'

'We all miss something at some point. That's why it's good to discuss, it's good to throw it at each other. Get different viewpoints, different angles. It's not a criticism; it's just what works.'

'Well, I've got everyone out to grab hold of witnesses. We'll advertise on the TV during breakfast this morning. We're doing stops in town asking people if they were in, a couple of car stops lined up, and street stops for pedestrians.'

'Good,' said Macleod. 'Now, I'll keep the brass off our neck.'

'Because?' said Hope.

'Because it's Christmas time. There's been a very bloody murder and we need to look like we're doing something.'

'We're always doing something,' said Hope. 'What do people think we do? Oh, look. There's a body. We'll just get rid of it. That's it. Don't want to spoil Christmas.'

'That's not the point. Be seen to be doing something. You and I know these things might not add up to much at all, and there'll be lots and lots of manpower hours for something that maybe yields nothing.'

'Well, as I say, we put out through TV and radio, and are waiting to hear on the street stops. The shop itself has been closed. That should bring people's attention to it as well.'

'Who's building the picture up?'

'Ross,' said Hope. 'Ross will cross reference everything. Use his team as he does.'

'What else are you doing?'

'Well, I've got Susan out pulling in the CCTV from the local area. See if we can spot anyone following Alice Greenwood.'

'Good. You throwing that at Ross as well? That's quite a lot.'

'No. Ross is not taking that. Paterson's going to do it. He doesn't know yet, but with him being confined to the office.'

'I was thinking about that. Do you think it's time he got out? He will not keep his career going being in the office. He can't be a detective in the office for the rest of his life.'

'Whoa, I don't think that's my call,' said Hope. 'At the moment, I'm told he's in the office. Therefore, he is in the office.'

'Do you think it'd be good getting him out, though? He had quite a trauma but he's going to have to watch where his career goes. To do that, he's going to need to go out to investigate. Otherwise, take the compensation and do something else.'

'Stop for a moment,' said Hope. 'Are we talking about the investigation I'm doing, or are we talking about just general staffing issues? If so, can you tell me because I'm going to go to bed and come back for the general staffing issues. I thought the investigation was important.'

'Of course, it is,' said Macleod. 'But you've got it covered.'

Hope almost recoiled.

'Did you say I've got it covered? When have you ever said I've got it covered?'

'You've got it covered. You don't need a net now.'

'Well, the Department seems to differ.'

'No, it doesn't. It's given me more roles. It's given me more work that's not frontline. Thinks I need to recover too, you see. They're not happy about my friend over there in the corner.'

Hope involuntarily looked round. Of course, there was no one there.

'He's just giving you a wave. I think that shows it's my mind very much that he's giving you a wave. The real guy, he wouldn't have given you a wave.'

'A guy who came after you to try to kill you,' said Hope. 'I can't see if he's giving me a wave, so it's not really bothering me.'

'It's bothering them upstairs, and that's why I think I'm being diluted more. Spread out so I can get less involved in doing the coalface stuff and more involved in the admin work. Look at this.' Macleod picked up a pile of papers to the side of his desk. 'What do I want all this nonsense for?'

Hope genuinely felt sorry for him.

'If you need some help, I'm happy to jump in. I won't jump over the top. At the moment, it's a straight killing, isn't it? Active rage.'

'You haven't read it that well then,' said Hope.

'I'm just telling you what everyone else has told me.'

'Alice Greenwood was stabbed repeatedly,' said Hope, 'once in the back and then lots of times on the floor. Vicious. Absolutely wild killing.'

'Random attack. We are looking at boyfriends and . . .'

'I don't know where we're looking yet, but whoever did it was able to sneak in. Whoever did it removed the CCTV camera to the changing rooms. Also, they may possibly have come in through the rear entrance to the changing rooms. Strange, that on a busy Christmas week, to have the changing rooms clear while they leapt in and attacked. Then they got out after a heck of a bloody attack, where they would've been absolutely covered in blood, and walked back out of a crowded Christmas shopping area. You're telling me that's a frenzied attack? There's too much planning going into it.'

'Or, they just got unbelievably lucky,' said Macleod.

'What? Did everybody turn their head as they ran out of the place covered in blood?'

'Yes, that was bothering me,' said Macleod. 'Anything else?'

'You haven't spoken to Jona yet?' Macleod shook his head. 'Well, there was a card left behind. It said on the card, "Listen, hear them ringing". That's it. "Listen, hear them ringing. Embrace your festive doom." Now tell me, does that sound like something that comes from a frenzy?'

'A card?'

'They had a card with them. Jona thinks it's homemade.'

'What? At the very least, premeditation is going on.'

'You're worried it could be serial,' asked Hope.

'There's no evidence to say it's serial, but there's no evidence to say anything at the moment. We can't rule that out. One attack in a Christmas period, the city could cope with one murder. Dark, yes, sad times, but it'll cope with it. It will go on. More killings start and people will get worried. They'll not come into the city. They'll spend less.'

'What about all the people that just died? I thought we solved it for them and those next on the list,' said Hope.

'You're not thinking, Hope. Of course, we do it for the people who die, and to stop others dying, but the city will kick off. Everybody will go nuts. You'll get people pushing at your investigation, telling you, "You need to do this; you need to do that because if you don't, their shoppers won't come back." Money talks, Hope. Even in the police force, money talks. That'll be my issue.'

'My issue is I also need to talk to Alice Greenwood's colleagues in the shop. She works in The Biz, that cheap art place, one that does the cheap remaindered books.'

'That's just down from the department store, isn't it?' said Macleod. 'Seriously.'

'Yes, but she wasn't on a break from work buying some shopping, because nobody at their store seems to have missed her. Nobody's rung in. I'm going to get somebody down there this morning when they open up because she'll not be there.'

'Check who knows she's on leave. Who knows what she was doing. Check any boyfriends.'

'Yes, Seoras. I know, I know. We'll go through all of that. What's bothering me at the moment is I'm not seeing a reason.'

'We normally don't see a reason at this point.' Macleod stood up, walked over and sat down in a chair in the corner, and stood up again and came and sat back down.

'What are you doing?' Hope asked.

'It's one thing they tell me. If he's sitting over there in that chair, get up and sit in it because it then enforces my brain with the notion that he's not there. Because if he was, I'd be sitting on top of him. Trouble is, he keeps moving.'

It pained Hope to see Macleod like this. She'd have given a lot more sympathy, except she was tired herself.

There came a bang at the door and then it developed into a steadier rap.

'Come in,' said Macleod. The door opened and a uniformed constable stuck his head in. 'Sorry, sir. Didn't mean to interrupt, but . . .'

'Seoras. My name's Seoras.'

'Yes, sir.'

'Not sir.'

'Yes, Chief Inspector.'

Macleod gave up. 'What can I do for you? It's Williams, isn't it?' asked Macleod.

'Yes, it is. I have a bit of information about what's going on.'

'You do?' said Hope. 'I didn't see you out there.'

'No, I'm about to head out and I told the sergeant because I saw some of the detail.'

'Which detail?' asked Hope. 'Who's passing details around?'

'We just got some of that message that was left on the card. People were asking if anybody knew anything about it. Well, I do.'

31

'Grab that seat over there,' said Macleod. He stopped himself from saying, Don't worry about the man sitting in it. 'Plonk yourself down and tell us all about it. Do you want a coffee, Williams?'

'No, no, Chief Inspector. It's fine.'

'What's your first name?' asked Macleod.

'Ian,' said the man.

'I'm sure you know Detective Inspector Hope McGrath.'

Hope reached over with her hand to shake. 'Ian.'

'Inspector.'

'No, no, no,' said Hope. 'I'm fine if you're intimidated by him, but I'm Hope. I'm leading the investigation, so you call me Hope.'

'Yes, Hope,' he said.

'I'm parched,' said Macleod as he walked through the door. He opened it, shouted out to his secretary, asking for three coffees. Closing the door, he sat down. 'Well, Ian.'

'Well, Chief Inspector, the thing is, the words that were used in the card.'

'"Listen, hear them ringing, embrace your festive doom,"' said Hope. 'Those?'

'Well, yes. I know them. They're from a computer game.'

'From a what?' blurted Macleod.

'A computer game. It's one of the latest ones. It's been out for a few weeks. They released it in the lead-up to Christmas.'

'What sort of computer game's this?' asked Hope.

'It's one of these first-person ones.'

Macleod stared at him. 'Where you walk around, looking from your point of view?'

'Sir,' said Williams. 'In it, the idea is that everybody's meant to enjoy Christmas.'

32

Macleod cocked his head to one side. 'Right. What's this game called?'

'Winter Slay Bells.'

'Oh, like the "Jingle Bells" song and all that stuff. "Dashing through the snow?"' said Macleod.

'No. Slay, as in S-L-A-Y—as in kill.'

'What?' said Macleod.

'Oh, it's an eighteen rating. Don't worry. It's comical, actually. It's quite funny.'

Macleod's face didn't show funny, but Hope decided not to stop the man in full flow. 'Tell us what you know of it.'

'Well, you have to achieve various actions in the game, and you're trying to sort out people who are not enjoying the spirit of Christmas. If they're really not, you carry out a murder spree, but as various Christmas figures.'

Macleod looked at the man. 'A murder spree?'

'Yes,' he said. 'I mean, it is quite funny.'

Macleod continued to glare at him. 'How's it funny?'

'Because it's just a game.'

'Let's not get caught up in this,' said Hope. 'Let's just get a bit more detail.'

'Well,' said Williams, 'you're making a spectacle of them because they don't like Christmas. You have to go on a murder spree, but you're trying not to get caught by the cops, and at the same time, you're trying to make it as public as possible.'

Macleod was sitting with his elbows on the desk, his chin held up by his hands, and his mouth wide open. Hope could understand this. Her partner, John, had a games console, and he played games occasionally. Hope would enjoy the odd one with him, but she didn't see Macleod as ever playing anything like that.

'Just go with it, Seoras. Who carries out these killings?' she said to Williams.

'Well, that's the thing. You've got Santa, you've got the snowman, you've got an elf, the Krampus—that's a Scandinavian folklore figure?'

'Yes,' said Macleod.

'Somebody called the Badalisc, who I know nothing about.'

'Spanish,' said Macleod. 'Bit of a strange one.'

'Yes,' said Williams, 'but he's got this incredible face with big red eyes. He's as scary as . . .' Hope watched the man suddenly slow down. 'Anything,' he said. 'Scary as anything. He's not the best fun in it. I've played bits and pieces, but I've not got that good at it.'

'I suggest you do,' said Macleod. 'I suggest you find anything related to the game that's of use, including the way the game is played and how you win, and bring it to Hope. Contact the game makers if you have to. I don't know if this has relevance or not, but it's too much of a coincidence.'

'Yes, sir. I will do. Hope, I'll get that to you before the end of the day.'

'Thanks, Ian,' said Hope, and the young constable stood up, making for the door. As he went to open it, the secretary came in with coffee.

'You can stay if you want for a bit. Finish the coffee I had brought for you,' said Macleod.

'I better get on shift.'

'This takes priority. Tell your desk sergeant that's from me,' said Macleod.

'Yes, sir.' Ian turned, came back, grabbed his coffee, drank half of it, and then made for the exit again. 'I'll get right on it.'

He opened the door, let the secretary out, and as he was

about to go, he stopped and turned. 'Oh, there's this one bit in it, apparently. I've seen it on YouTube. Santa throws people down the chimney. Apparently, it's absolutely hilarious. He puts them in the sack, he marches up, and just dumps them like he's dumping the presents down the chimney.'

Macleod looked at him. Clearly, the humour was lost on him, so much so that Hope nearly burst out laughing at Macleod's dry reaction.

'Any input you can give will be much appreciated, Ian,' said Hope. 'Get to it.'

The door closed and Macleod looked at Hope. 'Gone over your head?' she asked.

'To a large degree, but you don't quote texts like that for no reason. He said you must make an example of them in the game. People not enjoying Christmas. But to take that to its end.'

'What? Actually kill people for it?' asked Hope.

'Yes. Get into this quick,' said Macleod. 'If it's going to be a nutter, we need to know quick.'

'Will do, Seoras,' said Hope. She reached forward and drank all of her coffee, and then turned to walk out. There was plenty more to do that day. She should get down to the discount art shop. Murder based on a game—she was struggling to believe it.

# Chapter 05

There was something going on, Imran was sure of it. Sweeping up inside his freezer store, Bitter Sweet, he could hear the buzz. He'd gone home early yesterday, an issue within the family, and taken his young lad up to the hospital. It was nothing serious, but serious enough that it needed looked at, and so he'd come in early today.

There seemed to be a lot of police about for six o'clock in the morning. It looked like something down towards the department store. Imran was a fair distance from that. He went into the store that morning and started going through his books, checking he had his stock correct. It wasn't so bad in a freezer store, but he had a couple of perishable items he wanted to make sure he moved on. Having been in early, he was now feeling the strain on his legs. To stay awake, he had picked up his brush to sweep around the store. Some women had been in, picking up frozen items, and chatting away to each other. He hadn't understood what the excitement was about. They talked so quickly.

Imran was an immigrant from the Middle East, and had family in several countries. Because of issues at home, he had felt unsafe and had claimed asylum, bringing the family over to the UK. He got a permit to work, and secured some funding to get himself a small freezer store. That had been several years ago, on the outskirts of Inverness. Now he'd upgraded, in the sense that he was closer to the high street, but he was still running a freezer store. It worked well. His family was doing well, and he had reached his fifties. Did he miss home? Well, of course he did, but here he was safe, even if he didn't understand half of what they were saying.

Everybody just spoke so quickly. It was about the police; he could hear that. Something had happened. He was going to ask several of the customers, but he didn't want to engage them while they were in the middle of buying things. Once people got their heads together about what they wanted to buy, he didn't disengage them from it. Because if he did, they might forget, and then they wouldn't buy it and leave the shop without it. And that, at the end of the day, was the important bit. He was running a business, after all.

He wasn't one for the news either, or for the radio, unless the cricket was on. But something was certainly happening. Outside, the streets seemed to be busier than normal. And those passing through the shop seemed agitated. It was as if everybody was getting the joke, except for Imran.

He was always careful about what he said as well because Imran sold halal meat. As a Muslim, he never thought twice about it, but there were some who didn't like either the religious aspect or how the animal was killed. Imran wasn't sure there was a good way to kill an animal, or at least one that meant it was done in a friendly way and struggled to understand the issue.

After all, this was his faith, his religion. He wasn't deeply religious, but he went along with it, did what was necessary.

37

It was part of the culture. He thought you had to accept other people's cultures, especially when you moved in with them, but weren't they meant to accept him too?

He continued to brush the floor and watched as a lady made her way over to the counter, plopping down her basket filled with several frozen items.

'Lovely day, isn't it?' he said, as he rang her items through the till. He still had an old-fashioned till because he hadn't got an internet connection yet in the shop. It was enough having to pay for all these freezers. Also, the shop cost a lot of money due to its location.

He smiled at the woman, rang up the total, and then helped her place the items into her bag. 'Lovely day, isn't it?' he said again. She looked at him as if he was demented, shook her head, and left.

Imran hadn't a clue what had happened. All he had said was something nice, and it was a lovely day outside. It was cold, but it was sunny. He was always unsure of his English, never quite knowing if he'd come across correctly. English was a hard language. Sometimes people said the same thing, but in different ways, and it meant something completely different.

He picked up his brush and went back to his sweeping. As he did so, he saw a man come in. He was clearly from the local area, a white man, and Imran thought he looked like trouble. He'd spotted his shoes. They were fake leather, not real. In fact, he couldn't see anything leather on him. Nothing wrong with that principle, but the type who complained about the halal meat, they often were like that. Vegans, they called them here.

'See your meat, mate,' said the man.

'I'm sorry?' said Imran.

'Your meat. Is it food-safe?'

*The cheeky blighter*, thought Imran. *Is my food safe, my meat?*

'Look around you. See how clean the place is? It's very safe. It comes in frozen, and I keep it frozen. I don't let it defrost. Look! Look over there!'

Imran pointed at his food hygiene certificates. When he'd got the shop, he'd got himself trained up in the local way, but even back home, he'd handled food for years. It really annoyed him during the course, the way people looked at him as if just because he was foreign, he wouldn't have a clue how to handle food. He handled food all the time; everybody did around the world. If people kept getting ill because of it, you wouldn't be someone that handled food for long. In some parts of the world, people would take great objection to you, might even harm you for it.

'I''s not about how clean the shop is, though, mate, is it?'

'What do you mean?' said Imran. 'What is it you want?'

'I mean, is it really clean? Have you gone through and done it?'

Imran was raging. He had got the pest control people to put down all their traps. Gone through all the practises that he needed to. He cleaned down daily and had a deep clean every couple of months. Imran believed he went over and above because he knew that coming to a foreign country, people would be suspicious of him. So, he'd gone and done everything that had been asked.

He ran into the back and came out with an extensive file, throwing it down on top of one freezer in front of the man. 'Look,' he said turning the page, 'that's today. I checked today. Cleaned today. I checked the traps. Look, that is the pest control people. Look! Look, this is where it comes in. This is what I have sold, my stock take. I can tell you which stock has been there and for how long. I also have listed how long frozen stock should be kept. I have the temperatures of my freezers monitored. I know what I'm doing. How dare you come in like this? How dare you come in and accuse me?'

'I don't think that's the point, mate, though, is it?'

'What do you mean? Of course, it's the point. You people, your country says you have to do this. All this paperwork. All the paperwork is done.'

'Well, the paperwork might be done, but is what's in there what it says in the paperwork?'

'You idiot,' said Imran. 'What sort of idiot are you coming in here like this?'

He saw that a couple of old women had made their way into the shop and he tried to smile at them but his blood was boiling.

'You think that all of us around the world we don't know what we're doing. Only you know what you're doing. You bloody Scottish people, bloody British. You know? Everywhere else in the world. They know about hygiene too. They know about how to cook.'

'And everywhere else in the world, the same as here, people know how to bluff,' said the man.

Imran flicked through the pages of the file. 'Look here, sweetcorn—that's the date it went in. Those are the dates on the packets. Come here.'

Imran grabbed the man's arm, dragged him across the shop over to a freezer, and threw open the lid.

'There, that's that sweetcorn. Look at the date. Look at it.'

Iman picked it up and put it in the man's face. The man looked at it.

40

'Well, it's one item. Doesn't mean everything's like this.'

Imran slammed the lid of the freezer, causing the two old ladies to turn and go out.

'Now you're scaring away my customers.'

'I think you bloody well did that, mate, slamming freezers and that when somebody's asked you a normal question.'

'It's not a normal question. It's an assinuat . . . an asin . . . asin . . . It's lies.'

'Insinuation, and I didn't insinuate I just asked you to check. Bet you haven't got records for the halal meat. I bet you that hasn't been checked because that's your meat, isn't it? That's that funny meat.'

'It is not funny meat. It comes from cattle. Normal meat. It's just killed in a certain way.'

'And what way is that?'

'The way we have killed it for years.'

'Flipping foreign way; it's not our British standards, is it?'

'We have British standards to kill halal meat,' yelled Imran. 'It's slaughtered in the UK. It has to be done by the British ways. Same standard as any others.'

'I bet the cows don't say that.'

Imran was shaking, but he would not be beaten. He tore off into the back and came back with more files, slamming them down.

'Here, look, pick anything from that page. Pick.'

'I don't believe you, mate.'

'I said bloody well pick.'

The man pointed and Imran looked along the line on the page.

'That is in there,' he said pointing to a freezer. 'That one there.'

'Okay,' said the man, and he walked over and lifted the lid. Imran tootled over.

'Look at the paperwork. Look at it.'

He held it up to the man's face. Slowly the man scanned from the paper and reached down and picked out a packet of halal meat. He looked at the dates that were on it, looked at the codes and where they had come from, and slowly placed the meat back down. He then closed the lid.

'It's only one thing though, isn't it? Only one thing. You could scam me anywhere around here. You could be.'

'Check it all then, bloody well check it.'

Imran walked over, lifted a freezer lid, pulling out the meat that was inside, holding it up. Then to the next one, where a frozen raspberry lattice pie was held up. Then an apple one.

'All these products are safe. All these products have been accounted for. Everything is in the right place. You come in here like a bloody idiot telling me I don't know this, I don't know that. You are the one who should apologise to me. Look!' Imran opened up another freezer top, and then another one, and another one.

'Yes, but they're all the ones you're opening up. You haven't opened up that one in the far corner.'

No, he hadn't, and there was a reason for that. It was only half full, and it was stuff that he really wanted to get rid of soon. There was nothing wrong with it, of course. The paperwork was all still in place for it.

'You don't want me to see that one then, do you?'

'You can open that one. I don't care,' said Imran. 'Just make sure you shut it afterwards. As I told you, all the temperatures are monitored. I have checks being done on this.'

'We'll see about that,' said the man. He tore over to the large chest freezer, put two hands on it, and threw it open.

The man's face went into shock. He stumbled backwards. 'I don't believe it,' he said. 'What the hell are you?'

'Eh?' said Imran. 'What on earth?'

'I asked you what you are. I'm off to get the police. Was that you? Was that you down the road?'

Imran shook his head. 'What are you talking about? What's wrong with you? You people, I don't get your language. Why are you . . .'

'Evil is what you are, evil. Don't—don't do anything to me.' The man turned and ran from the store, grabbing a woman who was walking in, pulling her outside. 'Don't go in there. He'll kill you. He'll kill you.'

Imran was bemused. The man had shown such force to come in and tell Imran that his food was probably out of date. Kept going through every check and every piece of documentation that Imran had shown him, yet now, he'd simply run off. Imran did not know what was up with him, but he had left the freezer lid up. So, Imran walked across, put his hand on the lid, and went to close the freezer. But there had been something in there, hadn't there, that had bothered the man. He looked down inside the freezer.

Imran stumbled back and the freezer behind him hit him just below the base of the spine. The image in his mind of the freezer contents caused him to be momentarily stunned. He tried to breathe deeply. He hadn't seen a sight like that since—well, it hadn't been exactly the same and he'd left for good reason.

He put his hand on the freezer behind him, and tried to push himself upright. He said he was going to call the police—the man said the police. Imran walked forward again. He put his

43

hands on the edge of the freezer, let himself fall forward, and stared, looking inside the freezer.

Imran recited words from the Quran. He then stumbled backwards again before dragging himself forward. How could this have happened? How could this have occurred? He was here last night. He had looked in this freezer last night, hadn't he? No, he hadn't. He hadn't looked in this freezer for the best part of a week because nothing was in it. There was no need to. This food was going to be shifted on.

He tried to breathe deeply but then Imran turned to his left-hand side and vomited profusely on the floor. Imran looked down inside the freezer. It was a body, a man's body. He put his hand in, and tried to lift the leg, but it was frozen solid.

*Don't touch it,* he thought. *Don't touch it. You could put fingerprints on it. You could . . .* Then he looked more closely. It was a Muslim man. It was somebody from the community. He couldn't quite see, couldn't really register who it was, but he was one of his own and he was in a freezer. Somebody had died in his freezer.

'Allah, what had he done to deserve this?'

# Chapter 06

Hope had intended to go to the store that Alice Greenwood had managed, but took a phone call that directed her towards a frozen food shop. Bitter Sweet was off the high street, stuck in a back alley but close enough that it was frequented a lot by shoppers. It had a lot of cheap frozen foods, and Hope knew it well. It wasn't somewhere she visited particularly but if you were struggling on a Sunday for something for Sunday lunch, you might pick something up there.

Arriving in the centre of the city, Hope saw a large crowd at the end of the back street the shop was on. That street led out onto the high street and the city was abuzz with shoppers. Currently, a lot of them were crowded around a police cordon that was blocking off the side street.

Hope approached the cordon, asked to get through, and had to shove forcibly until she reached the front of it. The constable on duty pulled aside the tape and let her through. Susan Cunningham was right behind her, and the two women walked towards the shop to see the van of the forensic team located outside. Jona was standing outside it while a couple of her colleagues were working inside the shop.

'Turning into quite a bleak Christmas for many people. I don't know if he celebrated it, anyway.'

In the shop next door, which was a café, sat a man of Middle Eastern descent. Hope recognised him as the owner of Bitter Sweet and watched as he stared at a glass of water before him. He was accompanied by a young woman in uniform and behind him, Hope could see a woman in an apron bustling about.

'Got a man frozen to death in the freezer,' said Jona. 'From an initial look, I'd say he didn't struggle, but he's definitely been frozen to death. Been in there at least a few hours, maybe longer, but can't say. Underneath the body was a card.'

'Don't tell me,' said Hope. '"Listen, hear them ringing. Embrace your fest of doom."'

'Exactly. We're getting it down to a lab along with the other one. See what we can make of it. So far, the other one's been bringing up not very much. All the materials you could buy in any art shop. Handwritten. Trying to get the handwriting consultant onto it, but to be honest, I'm not sure it wasn't done with a stencil.'

'Are we sure he was dead today? Couldn't he have been in there for a while?'

'I think it's from today,' said Jona. 'From what the constables were saying, Imran, the shop owner had been in from the early hours of the morning.'

'What time does he open up at?'

'Eight o'clock, I think, but he'd been in from six doing a lot of tidying.'

'We'll talk to him ourselves.'

Hope and Cunningham walked into the café next door to Imran's frozen food shop. As she approached the constable, she moved out of the way and let them take the two chairs opposite the table that Imran sat at. He looked up immediately and although there were no tears in his eyes, he looked like a broken man.

'I'm Detective Inspector Hope McGrath. This is Detective Constable Susan Cunningham. We're just going to ask you a few questions. Imran, isn't it?'

The man nodded. 'Must have been quite a shock,' said Hope, 'finding someone like that in your freezer.'

'Yes,' said Imran, 'very much.' It was almost as if he wasn't present as he spoke the words. 'I was looking in the freezer because of that man over there.'

Hope looked over at the constable, who also pointed at the man. 'John Aspinall,' said the constable, 'is ready for interviewing as well.'

'Okay,' said Hope. 'Why was he asking you to see inside the freezers?'

'I get this at times,' said Imran. It was like he was suddenly returned to the room. 'It's because of the Halal meat. People don't understand Halal, some of them, animal rights activists, they come in and they say that the animals are mistreated. That's where he was going. He didn't say it exactly. He accused me of not running a tidy shop, not having food hygiene standards. I have all the standards the same as anyone else in the UK. Here in Scotland, I have the same. We have to abide by the law. We have to show our certificates. We have to record how things are frozen. We have to look after food the way you look after food. Everyone looks after food, but that man, he comes in ignorant trying to find fault because he doesn't like Halal meat. That's what it is. He is anti-Muslim.'

*Possibly*, thought Hope. She'd seen that a few times. She'd

47

also seen people overreact to it. It was one problem whenever you got angst between two nationalities or factions of people. There were always those others who reacted too strongly to people who were maybe asking quite civil questions. She'd have to find out if that was such a case or whether indeed Imran had been a target that morning.

'The man in the freezer,' said Hope. 'Had you ever seen him before?'

'He's a customer. I think his name is Sadiq. I don't know him, you know. I think he's Muslim too, but it's not like we all live in an enclave.'

'How often did he frequent your shop?'

'Once, twice a week, maybe at the most. I knew him to say hello to. That's how you put it. I must have asked his name at some point. He came in this morning, but he bought nothing. Then he disappeared.'

'Do you have CCTV?'

'Of course,' said Imran. 'I have to protect myself. I have it if you want to know how that man harassed me.'

'No, I want to watch the footage of Sadiq if that's his name, the time he spent in your shop,' said Hope. She watched Imran's hands. They fidgeted.

'Am I a suspect?'

'It's very early days,' said Hope. 'We have a man found dead in your shop, in one of your freezers. My job is to eliminate you from the inquiry. I want to know that he walked back out of your shop this morning. If we see the CCTV footage and he comes in and he goes out and then he doesn't come back in, well, then we have an issue. How did he get in? If something happened to him while he was here, it may clear your name.'

'He came in,' said Imran. 'I said hello. Good morning. He

was browsing. I told him I'm going into the back. I have to check some of my paperwork. The cricket was on. I stopped, and I listened to the cricket. I was maybe in there a couple of minutes and then I came back out and the man wasn't there.'

'The freezer he was in. Had anybody looked in that freezer this morning?'

'No,' said Imran, 'that's a freezer that's used for extra storage. I don't need it at the moment. It's away from the customers, in the store but off to one side. There's no see thru top on it and that's why it's my storage area. I have a big cold store out the back, but it was full, so I put some items into there. It wasn't full though.'

'How long have you run the store like that with a half-full freezer you can't see into?' asked Susan. Hope glanced at her, wondering where she was coming from.

'Couple of months,' said Imran.

'I think I'd like to check the CCTV. The Constable will take you through. I'll be in in a minute,' said Hope. 'Constable, Imran's going to operate the CCTV. He's going to take you to the point this morning where the man from the freezer—we think called Sadiq—has come in. Just observe him while he sets that up.'

Imran stood up, seemingly with purpose, and was escorted by the constable around to his shop. Hope saw Jona stopping them initially and redirecting them to go in via the rear.

'What are you thinking about,' asked Hope, 'with that question about the freezer?'

'It was not him. It was somebody else. Why in that freezer? Why in the one you can't see into? Two reasons possibly; you want the body to remain hidden, to be discovered later so you can get away. Or it's one you haven't been able to check, so you take a quick look, find it half-empty, throw it in. Or do you know it's empty? Have you been in before on other days?'

'Okay, good thinking. I'll look at the CCTV,' said Hope. 'Why don't you go out, get a canvas of this crowd, make sure we've got Uniform picking up anybody that was walking past this morning. People could still be out shopping. Many people make it a day. They may now wonder what's happened.'

'Will do,' said Cunningham. She stood up and walked out, and Hope watched the confidence with which Cunningham exited the building. Hope had that, and she was informed Susan had it too. Susan really was quite like her. They had called them the sisterhood back at the station. One of those nicknames you didn't really get to hear unless you listened particularly closely. Down towards the locker rooms, the guys would call them the sisterhood, but even the women did too. Plenty of worse names. Wasn't like she was called grouchy. Macleod got that.

Hope went to go into the freezer shop, but Jona redirected her around to the rear and soon she was sitting in the rear office with Imran looking at his CCTV screen.

'Have you run it through yet?'

The constable shook her head. 'No. I thought I would wait for you—the constable said to. Said it was better if there was more than her here.'

*Smart*, thought Hope, *just in case he's implicated and has to run. He doesn't look the strongest, but always best to have two if you're looking to apprehend someone.*

'Play it then,' said Hope. 'Don't stop it. I'll replay it or we'll lift it and take it back to the station if we need it.'

Imran pressed play and Hope sat through a few minutes. She could see Imran walking back and forward in his store, moving a few items. Then, someone came in, a Muslim man, and Hope thought it was the man from the freezer.

'That's Sadiq. He's talking to me there. He's asking about the cricket.'

'Big match on today.'

'World Cup out in India.'

'Okay,' said Hope. 'He doesn't seem to say much else to you. Just seems to look.'

'He never really asks. Some people are too proud. They want to find it themselves. Men mainly.'

*Doesn't change much across the continents, does it?* thought Hope. Then she saw Imran disappear. 'Where have you gone there?' she asked.

'Gone into the back room. Something's happening in the cricket. It was a close run out. They were going to replay, going to the TV umpire. That's why I was waiting. It was controversial.'

Hope made a note of that. She'd have to clarify that with one of the men. It was men that mainly listened to cricket, wasn't it? She wasn't being sexist in saying that. You had to be careful these days.

Hope settled down to watch, and her inner jaw almost dropped. A snowman walked into the shop. It was a snowman, wasn't it? All in white with the round head. There was a top hat, a scarf too, a carrot for a nose. It moved quickly. It didn't have twigs for arms, but the arms were coloured and brown. They were human, but looked like they had some sort of cloth over them with gloves on the end.

The snowman raced in and Sadiq didn't react before a cloth was put over his mouth. He went limp, and the snowman dragged him ever so quickly round to the freezer that he'd been found in. The lid was flipped up; the man was tipped up and in, and then the lid was closed. The snowman disappeared back out of the shop almost as quickly as he'd come in. Had he dropped something inside the freezer too?

'What the hell?' It was a constable beside her.

'A snowman,' said Hope. She thought about what the male constable back at the station had said. Ian Williams, that had been his name. He said Christmas figures and a murder spree. Hope had just watched a snowman come in and effectively kill someone. The tape was still running. Imran sat in a state of shock, similar to Hope. He came back on the screen on the CCTV footage and she watched as he looked around, a bit bemusedly. He picked up the brush and started sweeping the floor. The man sitting next to her wasn't saying anything.

'Have you ever had a visit before from a snowman?' asked Hope.

'No,' said Imran.

Susan Cunningham had been right to ask her questions. Somebody knew what they were doing. Somebody knew to go to that freezer.

'How long did you keep your CCTV for before erasing it?' asked Hope.

'Two days—48 hours,' said Imran.

'Well, we're going to have to hold on to it. We're going to have to see if anyone has looked in that freezer in the last forty-eight hours.

'We need to do some formal statements and that,' Hope said to Imran. 'We'll also need to take the CCTV. Your shop's going to be gone over with a fine-tooth comb by forensics. They won't take anything that's not necessary for the investigation. I'm going to get the constable to escort you back to the station, if that is okay with you. You're not under arrest, but I would like you to assist us with our questioning. The person who did this may have come in the last lot of days and I'll need to know about your conversations.'

'Of course, I'll help,' said Imran, but his eyes were still fixed on the screen. Hope turned to the constable and asked her to get Imran back to the station. On leaving the shop by the rear, she came round to the front to find Susan Cunningham talking to Jona.

'Anything useful on the CCTV?' asked Jona.

'You could say that. Make sure you do a good sweep for any fibres from costumes. White costume, top hat, scarf.'

'What?' said Jona.

'Also, take the CCTV in; take it to Ross. This needs to be looked at over the last forty-eight hours. Anything else you can get. I just watched the death of Sadiq on the CCTV,' said Hope.

'Who killed him?' asked Cunningham.

'Frosty, the bloody snowman,' said Hope, shaking her head. The other two women looked at her, bemused. 'Macleod will not believe this one.'

# Chapter 07

Hope spent the afternoon talking to Imran while Ross scanned the CCTV footage. Susan Cunningham helped Uniform pull together statements from people on the street, again to be fed towards Ross and to Patterson back at the station. A uniform constable was sent off to take initial details from the staff at The Biz.

Hope realised she needed to get back there as soon as. Was this one death separate from the other or were these both linked? The cards said they were, but you could get copycats. Hope knew she needed to hasten. By teatime, she was calling a meeting, pulling in the team and Ian Williams, the constable who seemed to understand the game. Macleod had come down from his office into the team room and was waiting when Hope emerged from her office, having got her thoughts together.

She looked out. The only person missing was Clarissa, which was a pity. She could do with the hound, as she liked to call her. Clarissa was Macleod's Rottweiler, or rather, she had been. There was no way Hope was going to call her that.

Susan Cunningham had been busying herself getting information slides ready while Hope got in her head about how she was going to play the investigation. With two lines of inquiry, she felt Cunningham was going to have to step up. Either that or Ross was going to have to be pulled away from what he was doing. No solution was ideal. You could bring uniformed constables in to help, and they were terrific, but she needed one of her own team to head up each line of attack.

She opened the door of her office, stepped through, and silence quickly took over. She appreciated that. That's what happened when Macleod stepped into the room. She hoped it wasn't because he was already there, taking up a position beside the filter coffee machine.

He never stood at the front with her anymore during an investigation. He only did that if he was leading it. It was good; it made sure they understood who was in charge. Although ultimately, of course, Seoras had sway over everything. Hope gave him a smile. He smiled back encouragingly, but she wondered if there was a man in a monk's habit stood beside her. Just what was Macleod seeing? She couldn't worry about that.

'Evening, everyone. Not what we wanted coming up to Christmas, but here we go. We have two victims. The first was Alice Greenwood.'

Hope nodded at Susan Cunningham, who took over.

'Alice Greenwood, manager in the discount art shop, The Biz, in the city centre. We believe she may have been on a day off, however. Member of a local church. She's also a spinster. Her life, according to reports from her colleagues, rotates around various church meetings. Some light sports activities, so we've got further things to get into there.

'We know she came into the department store, looking at new outfits. Possibly for an evening out because they were dresses. She got changed into some. She'd also got changed into underwear that hadn't come from that shop. Receipts for the underwear were found from a different shop. Possibly, she was planning a night out, something we have yet to find details about.

'While she was in the changing room, someone came in and knifed her to death. We think initially with a knife from the rear and then she was turned, forced to the ground and knifed on the ground. Copious amounts of blood were everywhere. The assailant was able to leave without being noticed, however. The assailant also took out the CCTV that was focused on the entrance to the changing rooms. The time slot from between Alice Greenwood entering the changing rooms and the attacker leaving is blank on the CCTV. Never recorded, switched off, but just that camera, so we're looking for someone who knew where the CCTV was and also how to operate it.'

'Are we focusing in-store then?' asked Macleod.

'Not specifically,' said Hope. 'We're going to trawl through the store employees. There is an exit out the back. A person may have come in via the front entrance of the changing rooms from the store or by using the corridors at the back. They wouldn't have been that busy. If you're a store operative, you wouldn't look out of place being there. We also believe that they may not have been busy enough to warrant being caught out if you used them.'

'How much blood was on the scene?' asked Macleod.

'Copious, Seoras. Copious.'

'If I may,' said Jona. 'Chief Inspector, you could not have walked out of that building without being spotted covered in blood. Even on a Halloween night, people would have thought it's suspect. The scene was covered. The assailant, if they walked out, must have changed.'

'Thank you, Jona,' said Hope. 'Our second murder was a Sadiq Muhammad, second-generation Muslim. Susan?'

'Thank you, Hope. Second-generation Muslim indeed. Worked as a manager in one of the large department stores. Family man, we believe, who came from his family that morning. Popped into the frozen food store, Bitter Sweet, on the back street just off the high street and was then shoved into a freezer by a snowman. The snowman then closed the lid.

'The owner of the store, Imran, was out the back listening to the cricket when it happened. He knew Sadiq. We cannot place Imran during those moments except by his own testimony. He then is seen coming back in through to the store and CCTV acting as if Sadiq has just disappeared. Not an uncommon occurrence.'

'So,' said Hope, 'we're looking at two deaths. Almost comical with a snowman involved if it hadn't been for the seriousness of it. The snowman clearly knows what he's going to do. He came in, he put a cloth over the mouth of Sadiq. He goes limp, he's dumped, and ends up in the freezer. Jona?'

'The man's unconscious as he goes into the freezer,' said Jona. 'Knocked out by the substance on the cloth. However, he freezes to death within the freezer. You would do. However, it would take several hours before that would happen. Most people would react. You would wake up. The sedative that was given to him was clearly strong enough so that didn't happen.'

'Imran says that's a freezer that he hasn't used for customers for a while,' said Susan. 'He keeps some extra stock in it because he's full at the back with his normal freezing storage. Having been there, it's not that big.'

'Why would it be? It's a frozen food store. You'll keep most of the stuff out for sale in frozen conditions. It's not like a supermarket,' said Hope. 'His story rings true. However, he would've known there'd been a space there. Anybody else would've had to check. CCTV is with Ross. Anything from it yet?'

'No one lifts that freezer in the last forty-eight hours before Sadiq's death,' said Ross. 'If they checked it, they've checked it in advance.'

'Nobody asked to dig about in that freezer. We have a John Aspinall coming in who finds the body initially. He's admitted under questioning that he came in to berate Imran over the sale of halal meat. Halal is obviously the way meat is slaughtered within the Muslim community. It's not something that is seen as appropriate by certain other parts of the community, and John Aspinall is an animal rights welfare activist.

'He has said specifically, he came in to berate Imran, trying to wind him up. He was also trying to have a go at him. However, he says he's never seen in that freezer before. He certainly wouldn't be putting a body in it, and the man seems visibly shocked. He's got no form. He's not seen on the CCTV looking in. And, Ross, do we see Mr Aspinall at all in the forty-eight hours previous?'

Ross shook his head.

'So honestly, in terms of suspects, we have Imran, we have John Aspinall, we have no link from them to Alice Greenwood. The only link between Imran and Sadiq at the moment, they're both managers. They worked in retail.

'It's Christmas time as well,' said Patterson. 'They'd be under pressure. Retail management is all pressure at this time. Do you think it could be about the store hours worked? Something on a human resources level.'

'It's worth looking at,' said Hope. 'And with that, I think there's two lines of inquiry we need to go down. The first one I want to look at is to do with cards that were left behind. At both murders, a card was left with a logo on it. The logo said, "Listen, hear them ringing. Embrace your fest of doom." The card itself seems to be handmade.

'As far as we can gather, materials could be bought anywhere at any art shop, although we'll look into it. However, that line comes from a video game. Constable Ian Williams is with us because he has played that game, and he spent today getting onto the creators of it. Constable Williams, tell us what you know.'

A rather nervous Ian Williams stood up and looked around him. Macleod was giving him a smile, but the presence of the Chief Inspector was obviously rattling the man.

'It's a game I've played recently called *Winter Slay Bells*. That's slay spelt S-L-A-Y. The idea of the game is that certain people have not been enjoying Christmas properly, and you have to carry out a vengeance on them. Ultimately, you have to kill them with certain Christmas characters. It's quite humorous. I was telling the Chief Inspector earlier, one thing you have to do is get Santa to capture someone in a bag and then dump them down a chimney to kill them. It's seen as a comical game, and that's the way its creators invented it. I think they'd be quite shocked to see how it is now.

'When you go on your murder spree, you have to do it with various Christmas figures. One of them is a snowman. You've also got an elf. Also a Badalisc, which is a Spanish Christmas time figure, red eyes, scares the children. You've got a Krampus, which is a northern European Christmas figure that punishes children along with Santa, usually with a whip made of birch. There's also a naughty elf.

'One of the things is that in the game, you get more points if you hold these people up as not celebrating Christmas properly in front of lots of people in the game. So, when you kill them, kill them out in the open and then get away with it. That's the idea of the gameplay. It's not uncommon; it follows a lot of other games where you get to be a character that you couldn't be in normal life. But, to be honest, I was finding it quite fun until recent events.'

'Do you think that the event in the frozen food shop would be something that would mirror what happens in the game?' asked Macleod.

'Yes, Chief Inspector, I would. Although, they wouldn't score that highly for it.'

'Score that highly?' queried Macleod. 'How? I don't understand.'

'Because they did it on the quiet, nobody actually witnessed it.'

'But they put it on tape,' countered Seoras. 'It's going to be watched over and over again.'

'Yes, actually, I think that is part of a game. I think there are CCTV cameras in the game, but not in the shop in that way, but I suppose if you extrapolate it, you could say that they're behaving like the game in that.'

'What about the other killing?' asked Macleod. 'Does that fit in at all?'

'It's very bloody. It's very bloody, and using a large knife. The elf is able to do that in the game. Also, the Krampus can use the knife, but it gets more points for the birch. The elf gets the big points for the knife and making it a particularly gory killing.'

Ian Williams said the last words slowly and Hope felt for him. He clearly had enjoyed this game. He clearly saw it as fun, and now someone was turning it into reality.

'When you play the game, though,' said Williams, 'you get to leave a card behind, and the message is sung to you. But you get to hear sleigh bells. You have to ring sleigh bells as you approach. The whole idea is you build up. So, when you do your first killing, you let the sleigh bells be heard. The people of the town fear the sleigh bells more and more, and then they end up turning their back and are more festive because they hear the sleigh bells.'

'That's quite a twist on Christmas, isn't it?' said Susan Cunningham.

'I guess they didn't think anybody was going to actually carry it out,' said Ian. 'It's a computer game. In computer games, we kill people all the time. It's also been shown that, statistically, people don't get more violent from them.'

'Thank you, Ian,' said Macleod. 'Don't beat yourself up on it. You don't kill people because of computer games. These people might not be doing it because of that either, although the game seems to be involved. You've been a great help, part of the team, just focus. The aim is to get the killer. Not beat ourselves up because we play a game.'

'Of course, sir.'

'Right,' said Hope. 'So that's a line of attack. We've got to see where the outfits are coming from. Let's assume that the first one might have used an elf. But otherwise, go across everything. I think Santa's the fifth figure in the game, isn't he?'

'Yes, he is,' said Williams. 'I didn't mention that. Sorry.'

'Not a problem,' said Hope. 'So, Ian, you're looking into that side of it. Report to Ross over that. He'll also get into that side. Ross is going to look after all the reports coming in from the street, pulling those together along with Patterson's CCTV. That's Ross's baby. I'm sitting over the top. Susan's going to step up and cover off our other line of inquiry, which is the retail industry.

'Why are these two people linked? We go out, we talk to their colleagues, we talk to other people in the shops. We need to talk to the trade, see if anything's happening. Is there anything kicking off amongst unions?' said Hope. 'Susan will use a couple of the constables, people out on the beat. So, thank you to the uniformed sergeants, and that, who are with us. Help is much appreciated.

'I'll sit over the top and do as I see necessary. I'm also dealing with Imran, who's currently assisting us downstairs, as is John Aspinall. We have arrested no one. Gut says it's not these two. There's no link to Imran and John Aspinall or Alice Greenwood, no link from John Aspinall to Sadiq.

'Coming up to Christmas, if it's tied into the game, I don't see this being done in January. We've got five characters in the game,' said Hope. 'I don't know if the killer is one person. It may be more than that. Maybe somebody or some group are playing the game together. I hope not, but we need to act quickly. There's potential we could be up against the clock on this one. Go to it, everyone. Thank you.'

Everyone stood up and Hope saw Macleod make a beeline for her. She waved him into her office. Once he'd entered, she shut the door.

'What? Did I miss something?'

'No, if you had missed something,' said Macleod, 'I'd have

told you in the meeting. You're grand. You're doing fine, and you're totally correct. We might be up against this. I'm here. Give me one line of inquiry. Ross has got a mountain to go through there. He doesn't need to be sitting on top of it. Let him deal with that side.'

'You can come in and take over, and I'll drop onto one of the lines of inquiry.'

'No,' said Macleod. 'You're the person for this. If I wanted it, if I felt it was necessary, I'd just take over, you know that. I'm here to help, like I said I would. I'll step in and help. Give me the clothing line, I'll chase that. I'll do the game as well. Monitor Williams. You haven't got Clarissa. You need another sergeant in here. Ross isn't that yet. Ross is still working and covering off all the usual stuff he does. We have not got a great timescale. You're right; this could be something that's serial and happening soon. Have people be where you need them to be. I'll drop in and cover. It's not like I don't know what I'm doing.'

'Are you fit to do it?' asked Hope.

'Well, he thinks I am,' said Seoras, looking past her. Hope turned and looked, and of course, there was no one there.

'I'm fit and ready to do this whether or not he's here,' said Macleod. 'I've been sitting on my bum since I came back. You need me doing this.'

'Okay,' said Hope. 'Costumes then, it is, and the computer game side. You've got it. Keep me updated.'

'Yes, ma'am,' said Macleod.

Macleod turned, walked to the door, opened it, then turned back. 'I felt for Williams. Do you know that? Frosty the Snowman. Christmas Elf. What's scaring me is we're going to have Santa running around potentially. Where do you find

Santa at Christmas time? He's everywhere.'

Hope nodded. 'You're right,' she said. 'I've got a terrible feeling at the moment. We're two down already. Potentially we could be a lot more down.'

'We're not two down,' said Macleod. 'We couldn't do anything about these two. The clock counts now. Let's go to it.'

# Chapter 08

Macleod strode up to his office, feeling more invigorated than he had done in the last month. He was back at the coalface. *Stuff the rest of it. Stuff the manpower reports. Everything else could go hang.* He was on the case. He was the guy in the middle of it.

It was true; it had been a long, long time since he'd been working for someone. Yes, he'd dropped down before for Hope on a minor case at a golf club. But this was more invigorating because this was out in the city, out on the streets. He waved over to his secretary, explaining he was going out. Macleod walked in through the front door of his office and picked up a bag with a laptop in it. He slung it over his shoulder, and then met his secretary as he walked back out the door.

'Where are you going?' she asked.

'On a case, unavailable. Tell them unless it's related to life and death, I don't want to be disturbed. If it's anybody from higher up, I'll catch them at the end of the day, unless the world's falling apart.'

'I've had the Assistant Chief Constable saying you need to be doing some more press. This case with two killings in Inverness—he wants to get ahead of it.'

'Route him to Hope. She's running it.'

'He's suggesting you should be.'

'I'm involved in it. I'm doing a lot of the spadework for her.'

'You're not stepping down to take over?' she asked.

'No, Hope knows what she's doing. She just needs help because Clarissa's not here. I'm covering.'

'You've got those expense forms to fill in. I've gone through them. I've done everything.'

'Do I need to do anything but sign them?' asked Macleod.

'No,' she said. 'Don't move.' The secretary ran back to her desk, then raced up to him with a piece of paper. 'Sign that and I'll fill it in. Get everything sorted for you.'

'Nice one.' He was about to disappear when he stopped and said, 'I may be in over Christmas depending on what's happening with this case.' His tone became serious. 'You need to have your time off. Okay? The next couple of days beforehand, cover me as much as you can, but you don't give up your holiday. Okay? If I choose to come in and work on a case, I work a case. You don't do the cases. It's not what you're about. You need your time.'

The secretary smiled at him. 'You've got something in your step today.'

'I've got murders to solve,' said Macleod. He almost skipped down the stairs. As he reached the bottom, he thought to himself, *Has it really got to that? The excitement only kicks in when I have people dead?* He looked across. Standing behind a constable walking the other way was a man in a monk's habit. He was nodding. Macleod ignored him.

Seoras walked out to his car in the car park, lining up his plan of action. He would go to his favourite coffee house. He would sit down and make a list of those who made costumes

66

in the area. *They'd have to be specialist costumes, wouldn't they? After all, there was a Krampus. You didn't get a Krampus in the UK. There was also a Badalisc—Spanish. You'd have to make that as well.*

Macleod stepped into his car, drove to the coffee shop, ordered a latte, and sat down at a table. He opened up the laptop, found the internet, and searched, pulling out a pad of paper beside him. He wrote down, over the next half an hour, eight different costume makers, more bespoke. Also, Seoras noted where you could buy costumes that were pre-made, scribing all the phone numbers that came with them. Soon he had his list developed, and he rang through them, ordering a second coffee before he did it.

As Macleod sat, there was almost a joy in what he was doing. You had to take a joy in it, after all. Yes, somebody had to die for him to go to work, but that wasn't his fault. If they died after he knew about it, well, then maybe he could take some of the blame for not performing well enough. The clock was on; the game was afoot. Just before he rang the first number on his list, he placed a call to his partner, Jane.

'What are you ringing for?' she asked him.

'I'm on a case with Hope.'

'I saw that. Two dead.'

'Yes, I'm hunting Frosty the Snowman, but keep that to yourself.'

'What are you talking about? Frosty the Snowman?'

'One of them was killed by a Frosty the Snowman. Hope needs help. We're down Clarissa at the moment, so I'm stepping in to cover.'

'Are you okay?' asked Jane. 'You're still in your recovery. He's still there, isn't he?'

67

Macleod noticed the man in the grey habit, who was strangely drinking a coffee at a table across from him.

'Oh, yes. He's still here. He's having a coffee with me at the moment.' Macleod thought this was almost hysterical. 'But he'll go. Don't worry.'

'I do worry. If this brings on stress, it could really screw your mind up. I've got your back, even if somebody won't leave us alone for our more exciting moments.'

'I've told you he will. We'll get there. It's best I get back to doing what I do, and this is it. I'm not running the case, just overseeing. And I'm simply helping Hope out.'

'Where are you then, if I need to get a hold of you?'

'Out of the office,' said Macleod. 'It's brilliant, but no phone calls. I'm just working on the case. Going through the old foot-stamping, trudging-along methods.'

'You sound happy,' she said.

'I am. I've got my phone list in front of me and am about to ring people. Going to see if I can find costumes.'

'Just be careful, Seoras. You know the people these things always end up with.'

'Better than you do,' said Macleod. 'It also might run into the Christmas hours.'

'I've never cared about that, you know that. You do what you need to do. My worry's about you, not when we eat our turkey.'

'I love you for it,' he said, in a surprising show of emotion. 'You realise that, don't you? I truly love you for that.'

'If you get rid of that stupid man in the habit, I'll let you show me.'

Macleod burst out laughing on the phone. 'I've got to work,' he said. 'You're outrageous.'

'It's you that has me that way, lover.'

He put the phone down and then noticed that the woman behind the counter was staring at him. He held the phone up.

'Just something funny,' he said. Macleod always found it quite funny that nobody really understood the way Jane and he were. He loved the fact that she could be a touch saucy with him, and out in the open. They worked well together, and Jane had a faith too which they shared. They shared a lot. He'd been lucky to find such a woman after losing his first wife.

Macleod picked the list of numbers up and spent the next hour ringing various outfitters. He asked if they had made costumes and then checked through the list.

One contact said, 'There was a woman who does party gigs who may be into more of that thing. She can do evil outfits as well as the nice ones. Jasmine's her name. A bit of an eccentric look, but very good at what she does. Jasmine Blanchard of Blanchard's Outfits.'

Macleod took down the address, and was advised that Jasmine didn't answer the phone during the day. He thanked the woman at the coffee shop, leaving a small tip, and walked back out to his car.

Blanchard's Outfits was on an industrial estate on the edge of Inverness, close by the river. Macleod pulled into the small car park and saw the rather cute sign overhead: Blanchard's Outfitters. The builders had seen fit to populate the industrial park with a series of green units, all with those corrugated roofs. The door for Blanchard's Outfitters had a simple sign on it, black lettering on white, but inside, lights were on.

There was a car sitting outside, or at least Macleod thought it was a car. It looked more like a hearse. The paint detail on the outside of the vehicle was amazing. Not quite to Macleod's taste, though. There were many skeleton skulls, but you had to admire the artwork.

He approached the front door, rapped on it, and then when nobody replied, he opened it. Macleod stepped through into a world of fabric. Shelves had fabric rolling off them. There were reams—is that what you called them? He wasn't sure, but the material was wrapped up around central poles.

There were offcuts here and there, sewing machines, and other type of haberdashery equipment that he didn't fully understand. There was also a rocking chair and sitting on it was a woman in a large, black skirt with Dr Martens shoes at the bottom. They were blue. On the top half she wore a t-shirt you would be more likely to see in the gym. She was a large woman, although Macleod wasn't sure she was overweight. She just looked big and, certainly, filled her clothing. Her hair was purple in patches, black in other places, and she wore pale makeup. Bare arms sported tattoos all the way down. Again, the artwork was quite amazing, even if the overall look didn't suit Macleod.

'Would you be Jasmine Blanchard?' he asked.

'Well, if I'm not, she's going to be mighty pissed when she comes back.' The woman laughed, and rocked the chair before standing up on the second time of coming forward. She marched over and held out a hand. Macleod saw the long nails, but he placed his hand in hers and shook it.

'I'm Detective Chief Inspector Seoras Macleod.'

'I recognise you from the telly,' Jasmine interrupted. 'Actually, I take an interest in some of what you do.'

'You do?' said Macleod, a little taken aback.

'The murders. The way people murder, I'm quite interested in that side of things. Fascinatingly horrible. Don't get me wrong! I don't want to be a murderer,' she said. 'I make costumes. You can see death's another part of us, isn't it? Why do people want to send other people on their way? Why? The whole Halloween horror type of thing, it's not like that. It's all a game, isn't it? What you do, it's not a game.'

*Game?* thought Macleod. *Maybe he should just pitch it.*

'Do you know anything about *Winter Slay Bells?*'

'Know about it? said Jasmine enthusiastically. 'It's a big hit. Very big hit. Very grotesque in the way it's produced, though.'

The woman said this without a hint of revulsion. She clearly meant grotesque in its genuine sense, implying how the art looked, how the figures were.

'So, I've heard. I don't play it myself. I'm not much of a gamer,' said Macleod. The woman laughed. 'The thing is, I'm looking to see if anyone has ordered costumes from the game.'

'Really?' said Jasmine. She had cocked her head more at him, staring more heavily with a right eye than the left, as if she was pondering something. 'Tell me more, Chief Inspector.'

'I'm Seoras Macleod. You can call me Seoras if you wish.'

'Never,' she said. 'I have a Chief Inspector here. Why would I call you Seoras? Chief Inspector—you should own that. Be proud of it.'

From behind the woman, a man in a grey habit looked at him. *Yes*, Macleod thought, *I should own that. I owned you.* Maybe that was a bit of an overstatement, but the psychologist said reaffirming that he was the one in charge was a good idea.

'Have you made any costumes that would be tied into *Winter Slay Bells?* I believe they have a snowman, Santa Claus.'

'They also have a naughty elf, quite a nasty one. The Badalisc from Spain and a Krampus. Funny you should ask, I have.'

'How long ago?'

71

'Completed maybe three weeks ago.'

'Do you have details?'

'Well, that's a question. I had some correspondence come in on email. Came from a lady, said she was gearing up for a party, but said she was shy, couldn't deal with people. I thought nothing of it. This happens. My trade, you end up getting people who are neurodivergent, or people who are certainly from different walks of the community. Some like to keep their identity quieter because of their lifestyle. For good reasons, not the bad ones like the people who keep quiet from you.'

'Go on,' said Macleod.

Jasmine turned and, with a finger, showed Macleod should follow. She took him through to a room in the back where there was a large desk with drawings on it. The current one had a spider, and it was being moulded into a costume somehow. This was then covered up by a large sketchbook that Jasmine flipped through. She pointed.

'Naughty elf, snowman, Badalisc, Krampus, rather suspect Santa. All done for that woman, all produced, all handmade.'

'Payment?' asked Macleod.

'That bit was strange; I have to be honest. Posted or rather hand delivered one morning. Came through with a note saying, "This is for all the costumes. Please deliver them to this address." She spent thousands of pounds with me, so I didn't quibble. I then took them and dropped them off at a house. To be honest, I think the house was abandoned. She didn't want to meet. Didn't want anyone to talk to her. Said she was too shy for that. "At this house, just leave the package. It will be fine." I didn't hang about.'

'Did you not find it all a bit strange?' asked Macleod.'

'A little, but I'm used to strange here. I get lots of uncommon requests. Most of them are not illegal. In fact, none of them I've had in the past are illegal. The money I've declared. I'm a proper trader, so I saw nothing wrong with what I was doing.'

'I'll need to see the email address.'

'By all means,' she said. 'I'll print everything out for you. Take all the correspondence. I've tried contacting her, when I've been sending other deals because a customer like that, you want to keep. Pays the money up front before you've even delivered the costumes.'

'You know what she was going to use the costumes for?'

'She said party, but it wasn't her going to lots of different parties.'

'Why?' asked Macleod.

'All different sizes, and from the measurements, one female, four males. I'll give you all those as well. I assume your guys could get a rough idea, maybe tell you who you're looking for.'

Macleod went on to his phone and pulled up an image from the CCTV footage from the frozen food shop. It showed the snowman just before Sadiq had come into the shot.

'This costume was used in the act of a crime recently. I can't talk about which and what or where. I ask that you do not mention what I've just said to you to anyone. Is that your costume?'

The woman put her hand to her mouth. She nodded. 'A crime?' she said. 'Murder. If you're here, it's murder, isn't it?'

'Give me everything you've got, all the details. It's not your fault, but please don't talk to anyone about it.'

'It's murder. Somebody used that to murder.' Jasmine began to cry. 'I'm sorry!'

Macleod wouldn't be allowed to clarify that. 'It's not your

fault, but help me. Help me now.'

# Chapter 09

Hope exited her office and shouted over at Cunningham. 'Time to go to The Biz,' she said, and then to the rest of the office, 'Anyone needs me, we're on the mobile. Let's go!'

'One second,' said Cunningham. Hope walked over to her and looked over her shoulder at the copious notes on her desk.

'What's this?' She said, firing through statements.

'We've got various statements saying what people were coming and going around the time Alice Greenwood was killed. Statements from the street. I'm just reading through just in case anything comes up when we do our questioning.'

'Good,' said Hope. 'Now come on. We need to go.'

'Okay. I'm on my way.'

Cunningham folded everything up on her desk and followed Hope down before taking the keys to Hope's car. She drove the short distance into the city centre, parked up, and walked through to the discount art shop that Alice Greenwood had previously worked at. There was a sombre mood as they walked in. The shop faced the high street with a large window showing a Christmas display.

Many books, discounted art sets for sale. Hope noted that

you could pick up a box of paints for a tenner. It was a large unit as well, folding out, showing you all different paints and pens. If you had nieces or nephews, it'd be the ideal cheap Christmas present to send them. Having none, she reckoned John wouldn't appreciate them.

Inside, there were books piled high in central aisles and stored on shelves at the wall, all discounted. Two for a fiver, four for ten pounds. She recognised the type of place. People bought a lot in here.

However, the mood was not jovial or Christmas-like. There were three women working. Two seemed quite old and were currently stocking shelves in different parts of the store. The younger one was behind the till and looked decidedly moody. Hope approached her anyway.

'I am Detective Inspector Hope McGrath. I'm here to talk to all of you regarding Alice Greenwood.'

'Terrible,' said the girl behind the desk, in an almost matter-of-fact way. 'We're quite busy at the moment. We gave some statements the other day.'

'I need to talk to you properly,' said Hope. 'I'm happy to do it here rather than at the station. I appreciate you still have a business to run. Can we go through the back?'

The girl shouted down. One of the older women came up.

'Hello, I'm Joan, and I guess I'm the temporary shop manager given what happened to Alice. It was terrible.' Hope could see the tears behind the woman's words. 'Of course, we can speak to you. We are quite busy though, so we'll do what we can. I'm happy to come through now and Rachel at the far end, she can come after, and last, there's Maddie here.'

Hope thanked Joan, and she was taken by the woman through to a small back room where they sat on plastic chairs;

Joan sat opposite Cunningham and her.

'My name's Joan Monroe, and I tended to cover the shop when Alice wasn't here. Just being the older woman, I'm fifty-two. It was a terrible thing that happened to Alice, on her day off as well.'

'Time off was quite unusual at Christmas time, wasn't it?' asked Susan. Hope reared slightly. It was quite an aggressive question to start off with.

'I think she had things to do. Most of the rest of us haven't had a day off this Christmas. We're getting time afterwards, which was all right. I don't have that much going on. I'm not sure about Maddie. Younger ones, they've always got stuff to go to, haven't they? 'Rachel has her family, but we're done by then. She doesn't have any kids, Rachel. Mine are grown up.'

'Alice was on a day off. She looked to be going shopping, and she may have been after fancy clothes, or rather trying on dresses that were quite glamorous. Did she have something to go to?' asked Hope.

'I think so. Understand Alice was a very quiet person. In terms of running the shop, she wasn't. She told you what she wanted. She ran it efficiently but outside of that, she didn't talk about her life. I'm not sure she had many people close to her. She wasn't a boss that shared a lot. She was fair in the main. Taking time off when she wasn't allowing us any, she must have had something important.'

'Did she have any men in her life or have any men that were looking to come into her life?' asked Hope.

'No.'

'How did she dress?' asked Cunningham.

'Modestly.'

'When she died, she was trying on some rather provocative clothing. Certainly, for someone who you say dressed modestly. Did you ever see her outside of work?'

'Not very often,' said Joan. 'Again, she dressed very similarly to how she was in here. She seemed to keep fit. Alice had the church. She was a Christian, believed in it too, but she was also a spinster. She did things like badminton, bowling. I think some of them were tied in with the church as well.

'Other than that, she seemed to rotate through church meetings. Whenever she said something to me, which wasn't often, it was always about going to the service, the prayer meeting, or whatever. I find it strange that she was wearing provocative underwear. I've only ever seen her get changed in here once or twice. Accidently walked into the room when she was getting changed. We are all girls here. It's not a big deal, and she certainly wasn't wearing anything provocative.'

'On the day,' asked Hope, 'did any of you leave the store?'

'Well, we're in sharp. I think it was eight-thirty we made it in for. We were here most of the day. I had a break, which was fine, but we had funny lunch hours and that was because of Maddie. Maddie had an appointment. She was getting her hair done. That was right. She'd been annoyed because Alice was having this day off when Maddie was getting her hair done. I told Maddie just to go for it anyway because she'd gone on and on about it.

'In the days beforehand, Maddie had gone on about not getting the time off, yet Alice was having a full day off, but we covered. Rachel's like that, you see. We covered. Get little thanks out of that girl, though. Bloody teenagers, eh?'

'Is she a teenager?'

'Maddie? She was when she started, so probably not now. No. She's been here a couple of years. She's worked in other places, in and around department stores and that. Knows her way around, handling a till and things. She's fine, but she's always that sullen. I guess she must be about twenty-three now. Still thinks she's a teenager. Everybody's a teenager when you're fifty, though.' Joan laughed.

'What happens now with the shop?'

'The owners have got to come and decide. Nothing's going to happen before Christmas. We're tied in, we'll keep it going and they'll look at getting somebody else in. They'll probably bring a temporary manager from somewhere else. Hard to do that at the moment with the Christmas rush, but we'll see.'

'Well, thank you for your time. If you can send Rachel in and then Maddie, that'd be much appreciated,' said Hope.

Rachel backed up everything that Joan had said and, like Joan, she'd been in the shop, only taking a minor break for lunch. Both of them had eaten there. Having finished with Rachel, Maddie came through. The girl had black hair and her face gave a sombre expression. Somebody might have thought she was depressed except she was belligerent with her answers. She had taken an appointment, gone to do her hair.

'Did you not feel a bit off?' asked Susan. 'The other two working hard and you're cutting right across lunch to go out.'

'It was the only appointment I could get.'

'Your appointment was when?'

'Eleven-forty-five,' said Maddie. 'It's a friend that does it.' Hope took a name. 'By the time she messed about with my hair and that, I had to get back.'

'Joan said you weren't thrilled with working every day in the run up to Christmas. You weren't getting any time off.'

'Alice was always like that. Then she took a day off. She had something on the go. You could tell something was definitely happening with her. I think she got involved with somebody.'

'Why do you say that?' asked Susan.

'Just seemed to always be—well, she was one of those church people, wasn't she, and then I noticed.'

'Noticed what?'

'She would wear slightly un-Alice things.'

'When she died, she was wearing quite racy underwear. Did you notice her ever wearing any before?' asked Hope.

'Yes,' said Maddie. She was getting changed when I popped in one day and blimey. I mean, she was wearing stuff for the boys.'

'What?'

'She was looking to hook somebody. I was quite surprised. She's that church-type person. I guess they aren't any different from the rest of us. I probably wouldn't have worn something like that, though. Boys got to like you, haven't they? Like you for you, not for what you can give them.'

Hope sat and thought about Maddie. She'd been out when Alice was killed. They would check the alibi for the hairdo. Hope asked her about what she was missing by not getting any holiday. Maddie reeled off a list of events. *Surely the girl couldn't expect to go to them all*, thought Hope. When she'd finished, Maddie disappeared off on her lunch and Hope stood in the shop talking to Joan.

'Quite a strange girl. She said to me she'd seen Alice wearing rather racy underwear. You just confirmed to me you never saw Alice change into something like that.'

'I never saw her wearing anything like that in here. Doesn't mean she never did, or she didn't get changed to go out. She was slightly different. If you're asking, did she have somebody on the go? Was there a man involved? I couldn't say that there wasn't. But if she was going to find one, I would've suspected it would be at these church meetings.'

'You said she was a spinster. Do you think she'd have any experience of relationships?'

'Not that I know of,' said Joan. 'She didn't talk about herself.'

'Did she ever talk about herself to Maddie, do you think? She wasn't like a mentoring figure, an older person to confide in.'

Joan laughed. 'Maddie and Alice didn't get on. Alice said this, and Maddie would do the total opposite. I don't think there was any love lost between them, but Alice couldn't find a reason to fire her. Maddie was always on about Alice wasn't doing this, didn't do that, and it was usually about time off. Maddie values her time off, but Maddie thinks you get time off every time. She thinks work should be suited to you. That's the youth of today, isn't it, though? I mean, you don't get to pick when you work your hours, do you? Bodies turn up, but you have to just go.'

Hope smiled more than the woman knew. 'Did you ever meet the person who did Maddie's hair, one of her friends?'

'No. She got off to sort her hair. That was it. On and on at me that day, that she had to get out.'

Hope stood looking up and down at all the books, wondering, and then Cunningham came up to her. 'I might want a quick word,' she said.

Hope thanked Joan, and together with Cunningham, stepped outside of the shop.

'What's the matter?' she asked.

'I've just seen Maddie leave,' said Susan. 'Something struck me. I didn't know what, so I grabbed the photograph of her, and walked behind her for a couple of streets. I then sat with the picture, looking at it, wondering what was bugging me. When I was going through all those reports from people who had been in the department store shop around the time when Alice died; someone was seen around the changing room area.

'It didn't say they'd gone in. The description was very precise, though. In one regard they spoke about the scarf the girl was wearing and it was a girl, but the hair wasn't black. The scarf had colours on it. Pink and blue, and I think there was a grey. It's a tartan of some sort. I can't remember which tartan it is. The detail's back at the station, but Maddie has one of those scarves.'

'Really,' said Hope. 'We need to check on that alibi. Maddie is an interesting person. We also need to get her measurements in case Seoras comes up with anything on the costumes that were made, if indeed they are made.

'I'll look into that,' said Cunningham, 'but trust me, she's holding something back. She also said that Alice had been seen wearing racy underwear. From the sounds of Alice, if she was having an affair with someone, given her church life and the rest of it, and the way she was around other women, I don't think she'd be wearing that type of underwear in the shop. Makes me wonder if Maddie's making things up.'

'It's an interesting thought,' said Hope, 'but we don't convict people of thoughts. Let's get some evidence, but that scarf really does interest me.'

# Chapter 10

'Thank goodness you're back, Seoras,' said his secretary. 'Had the Assistant Chief Constable on. He said the chamber of commerce folks are onto him. They're not happy.'

'Well, nobody's happy. We've got two dead people,' said Macleod. 'We are working on it. Hope's got it under wraps.'

'He wasn't happy you weren't here, either.'

'It's a time of change,' said Macleod.

'But you need to give him a buzz,' said the secretary as Macleod opened the door to the office. Macleod nodded, took off his coat, and hung it up before walking behind the desk. He cracked it. He'd got to the bottom of it, and he was desperate to speak to Hope.

'I'll give him a call in a bit,' Seoras said through his office door in the general direction of the secretary.

'But first,' his secretary said. She walked in holding a tray. There was coffee on it. 'Sit down and have one of these,' she said. 'Jane told me I had to make sure that you stopped every now and again.'

'Since when did my partner get to phone you?'

'Since you had your trouble.'

'It's not trouble,' said Macleod. He glanced over to the side of the room. There was no one there. He glanced to the left. There was no one on that side. Then he glanced back to the right. There was a man now sitting. Only moments before, no one else had been. He was in a grey monk's habit, and you couldn't see his face because of the hood. *Well, it's an improvement*, thought Macleod.

'I'll never leave you,' said a voice in his head. 'I'm here for good.'

'Will there be anybody else coming for coffee or is it just yourself? You have scheduled no meetings.'

'And I'm not intending to have any,' said Macleod. There was a knock at the door. Macleod looked up to see Hope standing, her head just below the frame of the door.

'I'll have one if you're making,' said Hope.

'Looks like I'm having a meeting. The boss is here,' said Macleod. He was in jovial form, something he wasn't expecting. Once the secretary had left the room and returned with a coffee, Hope took up a seat opposite Macleod.

'You sure you don't want to do this down at yours?' he said. 'After all, you're in charge of this investigation.'

'You're still the big boss and I still have to update you. It gets confusing this.'

'But before you update me, I know where the costumes have come from, even the ones that haven't been used yet. And there's five of them made.'

'Five of them?'

'Yes. Blanchard. Blanchard's Outfitters. Jasmine's a rather strange woman, but very helpful. She makes costumes and had an order for five. Strange orders. Someone who wouldn't make contact in a lot of ways. Eventually had to drop off all the costumes at an abandoned house. The money was dropped into her workshop. Cash. No way of tracing, but what we know is they're out there, whoever's done it. She's sending through the sizes and exact photographs of all the outfits. From what she said, we're looking at one woman and four men. All different shapes and sizes. Therefore, five different people in the outfits.'

'Five killers, or would-be killers. What do you think?'

'Sounds like a game, doesn't it, Hope?'

'Sounds like a pact. Like the world's gone crazy again. Are you buying that the game is provoking this?'

'I am,' said Macleod. 'The outfits are too much of a coincidence.'

'But what's the reason? People play games all the time. You don't decide, well, let's copy it and go out and do it in the real world. I mean, consequences for a start. There was that game where you ran around being a gangster and you were shooting people driving through LA or somewhere. It was like, okay, it's brutal but a lot of fun, but people didn't decide to jump in a car, get a gun, and start robbing places because of it. Why are they doing this?'

'I don't know,' said Macleod. 'But it looks like it is a game and it's on. Also, if they've got the outfits, it's probably going to happen before Christmas. That's what you have to do, isn't it? Protect the Christmas spirit. The festive feeling. Can't do that if Christmas is gone.'

'Did I hear that you're getting some pressure?' asked Hope.

'That's my business,' said Macleod. 'Focus on the case. I'm here to lift that off you, but do me a press conference, will you?'

'You want to be there?'

'No. You were always better at them. You're the glamour girl.' Macleod smiled. 'You know that, don't you?'

'I'm officially saying you can't say that to me, being your boss.'

'And as your boss, I overrule you. It'll keep them all happy upstairs as well. Female on the telly, all the agendas get covered.'

'And that's what it is, is it?' asked Hope.

'No. It's because you're darn better at them than me. Put me out there at the moment and one, I'll see somebody standing at the back in a grey monk's habit. It's quite off-putting when you're trying to make comments.' Macleod noticed that the man in the corner had given him a nod at that. 'And two, you just handle the press better. I'm liable to snap at them.'

'The other thing is,' Hope said, almost ignoring his defence, 'I've gone to The Biz, checked the people who work there. The younger one, Maddie Jefferson, she's a potential suspect. In fact, more than a potential suspect. Of all the staff who were there, and there's only three of them during the time Alice Greenwood was being killed, Maddie has no alibi. Well, she says she does but it's a friend who cut her hair. I'm not convinced, having spoken to the friend.

'I tried to lay it on but, to be honest, looks like a best buddy situation. Also, Maddie wasn't very happy. Alice wasn't giving her time off over Christmas, time off that Maddie feels she's entitled to, according to Joan, one of the other shop workers. I'd like to put a tail on Maddie. That's why I'm here. I'm struggling for staff. I will not stick one of the uniforms as a tail. It needs to be one of ours.'

'Susan?' queried Macleod.

'And then what? I have to step down and cover Susan's arm

of the investigation, or I take Ross out of what he's doing. I haven't got enough people without Clarissa.'

There was a banging on the door. Before Macleod could say 'come in', the door was fully open. In the doorway, in tartan trews and her infamous shawl, stood Clarissa.

'Am I interrupting?' she asked.

'You always interrupt,' said Macleod. 'Were your ears burning?'

'Why? Should they be?'

'We were just speaking about your absence,' said Hope.

'Absence no longer. Two bodies coming up to Christmas. From what I hear, we could be on to a serial killer. I'm back.'

'You're not back,' said Macleod. 'Go! Go have your Christmas, then get ready.'

'Someone told me you had actually dropped down and got out on the field again, working the streets. I'm not letting you have all the fun.'

Macleod stared back at Clarissa. 'I'm serious. You've got a new role starting up. You need to sort yourself out for that. Get your troops together. I'll be your boss, so it needs to go well. I had to fight for it.'

'You had to fight for it?' blurted Hope.

'Well, you never told me that,' said Clarissa.

'I am not obliged in my role as Chief Inspector to tell either of you anything unless it pertains to a case. I fought for it blooming hard, so have your holiday, come back refreshed, and make a success of this art gig thing.'

'Look, I'm here,' said Clarissa. 'Tell me you don't need me and I'll walk out.'

'We don't need you,' said Macleod. 'Go.'

Clarissa glared at him. 'Hope, tell me you don't need me, and

I'll walk out.' Hope hesitated. 'See,' said Clarissa, 'You need me.' She turned and shut the door behind her.

'I really could do with her. You know we could do with her,' said Hope to Macleod.

'As the Chief Inspector, I am advising you, Clarissa Urquhart, to have your Christmas and come back refreshed. If a lower-ranking officer feels the need to keep you in, to use up that rather generous offer that I'm giving, then on her head be it.'

Hope stood up, walked to the side of the room, and grabbed a chair, bringing it back to place it in front of Macleod's desk. Macleod looked a little quizzical for a moment because that was the chair that the man in the grey habit had been sitting in. He wasn't here now.

'I'll bring you up to speed downstairs,' said Hope, 'but I'm going to need you to head up one line of investigation. We are looking like we've got a serial killer on the go, except it looks more like serial killers and they're copying a computer game.'

'Winter Slay Bells,' said Clarissa. 'You'll find I'm a lot more clued-up. I don't come back and offer my services without knowing what I'm walking into. I checked if it was just something minor. As soon as I started getting information, I knew it was serious. I knew it could be long term, and I knew you would need the help. That's why I'm here, but before you ask,' she said, turning to Macleod, 'Frank gave his blessing.'

*Everybody always thinks of Jane*, thought Macleod. *Nobody thinks of having to spend Christmas in here.*

The door was rapped again. Macleod just shook his shoulders. 'Come in, why not? Anyone else?'

'Sorry to bother you, Seoras,' said his secretary, and Macleod felt bad. 'I just wanted to see if the Detective Sergeant wanted a cup of coffee.'

'Absolutely,' said Clarissa. 'I'll be staying for a while.'

The secretary shut the door, and Macleod settled back down again. Hope began running through the investigation with Clarissa, before the door was rapped again.

'You don't have to rap it to bring the coffee in. It's only us.'

The door opened, and Macleod saw Susan Cunningham. 'I didn't bring any coffee. Nobody ordered coffee. Was I meant to bring coffee?'

'That's another coffee,' shouted Macleod.

'What's up?' asked Hope, turning to Susan.

'Been to the department store where Sadiq Muhammad worked. Apparently, he's known as a stickler for the rules and there's been disquiet about how little time off for Christmas has been given. People are not happy, really not happy. Seems Sadiq is giving himself a lot of the good time off and others not. I thought you'd want to know as it's a similar connection to . . .'

'Maddie Jefferson,' said Hope.

'Who?' asked Clarissa.

'Maddie Jefferson works in the same place as Alice Greenwood. Wanted time off, Alice wouldn't give her it. There's a connection coming here,' said Hope.

'You've got the game on one side, and you've got this on the other. We've got five potential killers. How do you gather people together like that? What brings them together?' questioned Macleod out loud. 'Did they all just get together, annoyed they didn't get time off for Christmas? Oh, hey, let's dress up and kill people. It seems a little extreme.'

'I've seen worse,' said Clarissa.

'You will not get this one, Macleod.' Macleod looked back over towards the side of the room where the chair had been and now, standing upright, was the man in the grey monk's habit.

'Shut up, you,' said Macleod to the wall.

'What?' blurted Clarissa.

'You'll get used to that. He's still seeing the people,' said Hope.

'The person,' said Macleod. 'Just the one person, but I'm fine.'

'You were going to stop me from coming back?' said Clarissa indignantly.

'Right,' said Macleod. 'This is Detective Inspector Macleod's office. It's not a free-for-all. Hope, bring Clarissa up to speed when you go downstairs. Cunningham, if the Detective Inspector hasn't anything further for you, back out you go. Thank you very much.'

Hope told Cunningham to take Clarissa downstairs and, as the sergeant was coming back, to brief her on everything that had happened. The women stood up, walked out of the door which then shut, and was then rapped upon a minute later.

'What?' shouted Macleod. The door opened, and the secretary stood with several coffees.

'Downstairs, murder squad office. They've gone back down there. Sorry. Thank you,' he said. The door shut again, and Macleod sat back in his chair.

'You came in to ask me for help.'

'That I did,' said Hope, 'and it looks like I've got it. But your question, how would you bring people together? We'll start looking into the staff at Sadiq Muhammad's to see if there are any gamers, to see who's kicking off the most. I'm going to put a tail on Maddie, and I'm going to use Clarissa for it. We don't have time to mess about. The next killing could be tonight, tomorrow morning, the next day or two. Christmas Eve is not far away. Time to put somebody on who can shake a person up.'

'Good idea. Has Ross come up with anything yet?' asked Macleod.

'He's got such a sea of work to get through, videos, reports, but Cunningham came up with the Maddie Jefferson bit. She was wearing the same scarf as we'd seen outside the changing rooms. We're getting there. You always said that the start was like this. It was a scramble. It was running around in the dark. You had to find that first thing and then it built, and then it went.'

'We usually have a bit more time,' said Macleod. 'We've got a clock on us. A clock that we don't know when it will chime. It's like trying to defuse a bomb without a timer.'

'But we'll get there,' said Hope. 'We've got the entire team on it. Everybody is pulling. We'll get there, Seoras.'

'I know we will. It's never in doubt,' said Macleod. 'Go prep your news briefing. I'll come down in a bit and you can just run me through it before you do it, and then I get on.'

'I'll do my best, but honestly, you may need to run cover for me. We're going to have so much going on. We're going to take flack and we're going to take phone calls from everyone and his aunt this time. If these murders continue and shoppers are put off, there'll be trouble. Sadiq, Alice, they're decent ordinary people, by the looks of it, at least on the outside. Papers will run that; the TV will say that. Random killings. People will stop shopping.'

'I remember a time,' said Macleod, 'when Christmas was about a child in a manger. It was about family coming together. A celebration, whether you believed or not, about going to places together, singing together. It wasn't about buying stuff.'

'Come on, Seoras,' said Hope. 'You're not that old.'

# Chapter 11

Alan Ross stared at the myriad of pieces of paper in front of him, then turned and looked at the whiteboard behind him. He was flanked on either side by uniformed constables who were helping with the investigation, as was the nature of his process. He'd divided up the various reports, asking his colleagues to pull his attention towards anything, even if minute.

The witness reports referred to activity before and after the murders, around the shopping centre, in the streets outside, and from those who had visited the frozen food shop. The trick was to get rid of all the rubbish—the well-meaning, well-intentioned things. To lose the normal, everyday occurrences, and try to find those that stuck out. That wasn't easy. The problem Ross had was he never seemed to get the same constables on either side to work with.

'I think I've got something,' said the young woman sitting beside Ross. He walked over, crouched down beside her chair, and looked at the piece of paper she was holding in her hand.

'What is it?' asked Ross.

'Well, I've got a report of a man who seemed quite annoyed when he was out in the street.'

'How close is it to the incidents?'

'After the second one, the frozen food shop.'

'Based on which timing? The timing when he's pushed in or the timing when he's found?'

'When he's pushed in. It's between that and when we actually found the body,' said the constable.

'Okay, and what do you have?'

'A guy sitting on the street, fiddling with a carrot.'

'Fiddling with a carrot?'

'Yes, it's quite funny, because it says he was fiddling with a carrot that seemed to have a dent in the top. Not something you really do, is it, in the street? Play with a carrot?'

'The snowman that carried out the killing had a carrot nose. I see where you're coming from,' said Ross. 'Who was the person who saw it?'

'Jimmy Chambers. Oh, hang on a minute. You may not want to take this too seriously. I know Jimmy Chambers. Pulled him in a few times. He's been on to social services. Bit of an alcoholic. Sad case really. Only child died. Him and the wife split up. He's more often pickled than sober.'

'Where was the man having the carrot, though? How far away from the shop?'

'Five hundred yards?'

'Anybody else see it? Any other reports?' Ross stopped to put his hand up. 'Everyone, any other witness reports about someone handling a carrot?'

Bemused looks were focused on Ross. Then again, they were fairly used to this. How many times did he put his hand up and stop them, asking if anybody else corroborated something that was happening?

*Why would you be looking at a man holding a carrot unless you were a drunk? Was that the case? Is that why no one else noticed?*

Nobody came back saying any of the other witness statements talked about a carrot, and Ross was almost ready to leave it. Instead, he took a look at the footage of the death of Sadiq again.

Ross sat down in front of his screen and began running the footage. He watched as the snowman rushed in, grabbed Sadiq Muhammad, and pushed him into the freezer, before placing the lid down quietly and then exiting. The carrot seemed all right at first. Nothing peculiar about it.

Ross activated some measuring tools on the screen. He captured the distance that the snowman was from the screen on the way in and he measured the length of the carrot nose. He then, once the murder had been committed, stopped the footage of the snowman on the way out at approximately the same rough position. Ross was fortunate to find the nose in profile again and took another measurement.

According to these calculations, the nose had grown smaller. Ross could feel the adrenaline picking up inside him. There was nothing guaranteed about this. Nothing that said this was a definite path to be following. After all, he was measuring carrots on a screen; that was liable to error, wasn't it? There was a definite decrease in the carrot's size. Not massive, but definitely something.

Ross picked up his desk phone and dialled the number for the forensic lab, where he asked to speak to Jona Nakamura.

'Jona, it's Ross. I need to know something. Did you keep the contents of the freezer, the one that the body was found in?'

'Yes,' said Jona. 'Of course, we have, at the moment. We've got the whole freezer as well, but because it's defrosted, we scooped up the contents. It's mainly old bits of vegs sitting in our freezers.'

'Okay,' said Ross. 'Do you have any carrots amongst it?'

'Yes, there were carrots stored in that freezer in the boxes underneath, and there were some boxes outside, though, as well. There are definitely carrots about in the store, too. Pretty common.'

'I've got a theory, but I'm not sure if we can corroborate it.'

'Well, hit me,' said Jona, 'and I'll tell you.'

'I've measured the size of the carrot on the snowman figure coming in and going out, and it appears that it's decreased. I think some of the carrot may have been knocked off. Maybe it had been loose or whatever, but I think it may have dropped into the freezer.'

'Okay,' said Jona, 'but we got a freezer full of carrot underneath in boxes. I'm not so sure that we can pick it out. I'll have to talk to someone. That's if we even find the right bit of carrot to begin with.'

'You have a look at them, and I'm going to come over. Let's see what we can do.'

Ross put the phone down, turned to one constable, advising him where he was off to, and told him to contact him immediately if anything came up. He walked out of the main office, but as he passed the door of Hope's office, he heard it open.

'Where are you off to?' she asked. 'Anything good?'

'Don't know yet. Going to look at carrots.'

'What?'

'See if Frosty the Snowman left anything behind. I won't be long.'

Ross continued out of the office and walked through to the forensic department on the other side of the building. He knocked on the door and opened it. He saw Jona on the far side of the room, waving at him.

'Stick a lab coat on, but over here.'

When Ross arrived to where Jona was, he saw a metal table in front of him with an array of bits of frozen vegetable.

'That's the contents of the bottom of the freezer. We're going to pick out all the carrot and see if there's any difference to the carrot that was stored in the bottom. That's the first step.'

'Okay,' said Ross. 'Go on then.'

He stepped back, watching with intrigue as Jona and a colleague sorted through, taking out all the bits of carrot and putting them to one side. It took the best part of twenty minutes. The rest of the sample was carefully replaced back in a bag and put back into storage while Jona scanned over the carrots.

'You can come in closer,' she said. 'Look. See that one there? It's a slightly different colour variation, as is that one and that one. That looks like an end piece, as does this one.'

'Are they any different?' asked Ross. 'I know you've said the colour's different, but can it be from a different type of carrot? Are they all the same? What varieties?

'Whoa,' said Jona, 'slow down. I need to get a hold of somebody who actually deals with carrots. Methodology and process I can do. I can tell you how to differentiate stuff. I need somebody who actually knows about carrots to inform me about varieties. We're phoning around a few farmers and processors.'

'I've just been thinking,' said Ross, 'that if you were going to get a carrot, where would you get it from for your nose? Would you buy it from a supermarket? If you did, you'd be on CCTV buying carrots.'

'People buy carrots all the time. That'd be an enormous amount of work to find someone amongst all those people.'

'Of course. But would you take it from somewhere where you will not be filmed? If you're murdering someone, you'd do a great job of covering yourself as you do it. The last thing you need is to be on camera anywhere.'

A colleague of Jona's came up to her and whispered something in her ear.

'I think you should do whatever you do for another hour. I've got a man coming in who I need to talk to. Then hopefully, I'll have something for you. There's definitely a different carrot in here,' said Jona. 'Whether it belongs to yours in the video is another matter.'

Ross made his way back to the main office and sat down, going through his witness statements again. There'd been a few more links passed through. Someone had seen a person with an umbrella near the changing rooms. The umbrella had looked fat. However, in calling the witness, said umbrella had been discovered and you couldn't hide anything in it.

These were normal things. Normal first impulses to go through. Ross's mind was back on the carrot. The carrot was more than a first impulse. There was a carrot actually involved in the murder. Therefore, this could be a potential lead if they could isolate the carrot. Ross resisted the urge to look at carrots and what varieties they were, and how you would differentiate between them.

You had to let Jona do what she did. She didn't become a detective, or put together the evidence. She told you what she found. You could ask her to discover what certain items were or what was special about them or not. She never turned around and solved things for you. She simply said what was.

You had to put the pieces together. Ross thought it only fair that you didn't step on her territory either.

As he sat there, Ross watched Clarissa come in, plunk herself down in her seat, look up at the computer and then go to leave.

'What are you doing here?' he asked.

'In on the case. Off to tail someone. Better bring a Rottweiler in when it's needed,' said Clarissa, laughing.

Ross thought that was quite unusual. She didn't usually like the term, snarling at people who said it and giving all the more reason for it to be announced as her name. It would be good, though, to have her on the team again.

'Have you got anything for me, Als? I heard you were after Frosty the Snowman.'

'Possibly,' he said. 'Don't cause too much fuss.'

'You know me, Als,' said Clarissa. She swished her shawl around her shoulders. 'Always ready for the fight.'

The last sentence was said with less aplomb than Clarissa usually spoke. He wondered if she'd come back out of the sense of duty rather than desire. She'd been hit hard, and he noticed she glanced across at Patterson before she left the room.

Ross's phone rang. He picked it up, heard Jona speak, and told her he'd be over instantly before she'd even finished the sentence. He fought the urge to almost skip out of the office, and within two minutes was standing inside Jona's, looking at a man with a weathered face and greying hair.

'This is Jeremy. Many years in the agricultural business,' said Jona. 'This piece of carrot in front of me, it's a different variety.'

'Very special one that,' said Jeremy suddenly. 'Not grown in many places. You wouldn't get that unless you'd sent off for the seeds from specialist growers. Kind of thing that people like to do in their greenhouses. Special thing. Also coming to fruition later round about November time. As a variety, it would be of the correct size for the nose. It would be available in greenhouses, but you wouldn't buy that in a supermarket.'

Ross turned to Jona. 'If I could find you the carrot of the snowman outfit, would you be able to match that piece to it?'

'We could give it a go, but who knows if it's been damaged? We could match the carrot type, the variety.'

'How rare would you say someone growing that variety up here would be?'

'I'll get on to those who supply it. You've maybe only got a hundred people in the UK growing these.'

'It's not a definite admission of guilt,' said Ross, 'but it could certainly be tied to it.'

'Did the costume come with a carrot from the maker?' asked Jona. 'I thought the boss had traced the outfits.'

'No, the carrot's fresh. That was part of the look. Thank you, sir,' said Ross, putting a hand over.' Jeremy shook it. 'I'll need to know who supplies these carrots. If you wouldn't mind coming back to the office with me, I'll sit down and make a note.' Ross turned and showed the man towards the door. As he turned away, he heard Jona laugh.

'What's up?' asked Ross.

'You're hopping about now like the Easter bunny.'

'It's the wrong season,' said Ross. He gave a grin. 'There can't be that many people growing these carrots. If it's only a hundred across the UK, how many are going to be up here in the Highlands? If someone's nicked a single carrot to go in front of the costume, might give us an area. It might give us the person, or someone the person's in contact with.'

Jona smiled and turned to place the evidence away again.

'Go hunt your carrots,' she said. 'Hop it.'

Ross turned around and dropped one shoulder to give a disparaging look with his eyes. 'Seriously?' he said. 'That's the best you've got for me?'

'Next time you come in here it'll be, "What's up, Doc?"'

# Chapter 12

Inverness was buzzing with the Christmas feeling. It was the last week before Christmas, a time when shops were desperate for people to come in and clean out their shelves. The festival of picking presents and spending money that people didn't really have. In truth, though, there was a good buzz about the town although there had been two murders.

The public didn't know the genuine horror of what had gone on. One had taken place inside changing rooms and the scene had been cordoned off before too many people had seen it. The death in the freezer shop had little gore to it and hadn't really attracted that much attention. The police hadn't released the fact that there was a snowman involved.

The large stage in the city centre was tonight going to be host to an award ceremony. Local radio celebrity, Angus McTavish, was to present various heroes of the community with awards. There was a band playing, music thumping out, and various street traders were supplying the cold public with hot treats. There were chestnuts, burgers, pulled pork in a bun with apple sauce, mulled wine, here and there, as well as the usual throngs of candyfloss and chippy vans.

As people went here and there, there was a quiet undertone about the killings. The genuine worry about it was amongst the shopkeepers and those of the town who would lose out from trade in this coming week. Times had been hard across the country, but Christmas time was when people spent, when they indulged, when the traders would make up for earlier losses.

'Well, what about that then?' said Angus McTavish.

He was a small man dressed in tartan trews, a flat cap on his head, and a Scotland scarf around his neck. He had fingerless gloves on and was jumping around the stage because he was cold. The backdrop behind him with the large chimney on the houses had sparkling lights across the top of it. McTavish whipped the crowd up into a frenzy before introducing some Highland dancers and then raced off to the side of the stage to grab hold of a cup of coffee.

'I'm freezing my bollocks off up there. Is this the awards crowd?' he asked, looking at various people standing around backstage.

'This is it,' said the stage manager. 'So, you've got five to give out. They're all on the cards here. All you've got to do is say the bit. They'll come on stage, and I'll have the awards coming in from the other side. Just make sure you bend down with the kid in the wheelchair. Don't stand upright, it won't look good.'

'I've been doing this for a while, you know,' said Angus. 'We'd better get on with it soon. I'm going to be dying for a pee. It's Baltic out here, isn't it?'

Angus turned and saw two women beside him, maybe in their early twenties. They were both dressed in Santa Claus outfits, except instead of beards they simply had red hats on their heads. The jackets also stopped around about mid-thigh, showing off legs and sheer tights.

'I take it you girls are bringing the awards on to me?'

'Yes,' said Emma. She was a brunette and put her hand forward for Angus to shake. 'I'm Emma,' she said. 'This is Jilly.'

'They could have given you a pair of trousers,' said Angus. 'I'm frozen in this.'

'Yep,' said Emma, as she jumped up and down. A piper was blaring away as the Highland dancers continued, and Angus truly thought he was going to need the toilet. He got the nod from the stage manager, and up he jumped onto the side of the stage.

'What about that, then? That's how you do Christmas in the Highlands,' he shouted. 'Ho, ho, ho.' He turned and put his hands up for the crowd. There was a poor response.

'I said ho, ho, ho, and you say Merry Christmas.' He did it again. 'Ho, ho, ho.'

'Merry Christmas,' came the shout.

'That's better. Let's have a big round of applause for our dancers.' Angus strode across the stage, clapping away, and then found a spotlight shining on him. 'We've got some awards to hand out tonight, and the first one's going to go to a very special guy.'

Angus wittered on for the next thirty seconds about the fundraising efforts of a boy who had been reduced to going about in a wheelchair because of a car accident. Angus gave a thunderous round of applause. The crowd joined in as the young man wheeled himself on stage, accompanied by Emma, with a large plaque. Angus took the plaque, placed it with the boy, and crouched down beside him while photographs were taken.

After that, he gave an award to an old lady who hobbled across the stage. She'd done forty years of volunteering, and Angus gave his best smile while Jilly froze beside them as she presented the plaque over.

The next one was for a man called Ernest Lyle. He looked a bit bemused as he took to the stage, and Emma had to bring him across. Angus could hear sleigh bells being rung somewhere, the sound rising in volume. The man seemed to look back in the wings several times. The entire scene looked a bit off, so Angus gave a 'Ho, ho, ho,' to the crowd who gave a, 'Merry Christmas' back. As they did so, a figure approached the stage from the far side.

*What the hell's that?* thought Angus. *It's weird. It's more like Halloween.*

A horned figure had climbed up on the stage. It was black with a long tail behind it. It also looked like it had hooved feet, but there must have been some shoes underneath that. Angus thought someone had got the wrong time of year. Why would you have something like this? Who in their right mind would dress up in this way at a festive shindig?

The horns were a work of art, curling and spiralling away from the head, and the eyes looked positively evil. There was fur hanging down off the jowls of the creature, and a pair of sharp fangs came out of its mouth. One thing was obvious: it could actually move easily, despite the elaborate get-up the person was wearing.

Angus glanced over at the stage manager, who simply shrugged her shoulders. Emma looked nervous beside him, and then Angus noticed the figure was also holding what looked like a large branch. Or was it? Because the creature was swishing it about.

Angus remembered being young. There was a time when in the private schools, canes could still be used. Not that often, but he'd received a few hits to the hand. The swish of the piece of wood the figure was holding brought back some painful memories.

'What's all this then?' said Angus cheerfully. 'Who's this figure?'

There were shouts from behind. Calls from the crowd. Somebody said something like the word Kampus. *A Kampus? What on earth was a Kampus?* thought Angus. The crowd were dressed up. Not everyone, but there were many Santa Clauses, snowmen, and elves. There was the odd reindeer. And yes, there were some figures like this, not many.

Angus had thought it strange, but this one was superb. This outfit was quite stunning. But now the figure was stalking across the stage towards them. But more than that, the wooden cane or whip, as it was, was being cracked on the floor of the stage. The metal ringing as the creature stomped towards them. *It wasn't a creature, though,* thought Angus. *That's a person. What are they doing?*

He turned, looking for the security staff, but he couldn't see any. The figure lurched forward, running towards them, and Angus stepped in front of Emma. She screamed, holding him by the waist. He thought about hiding behind her.

The hoofed figure ran towards them. It didn't raise up its whip though. Instead, it simply pushed out with its left hand, knocking Angus backwards. He fell into Emma, and the two of them went to the floor of the stage, landing on their backsides. Ernest Lyle was left standing on his own, and the figure whipped him hard with the rod he was carrying. Angus was shocked as blood appeared on the man's trousers, and then across his face as the figure went at him again and again.

McTavish had seen a lot in his time, and now, though he was older, he still was brave. He'd fought for his country, always a military man, and he wouldn't let something like this go without being checked.

He had hoped the security staff would be there. After all, they were younger, more capable of handling someone like this. But that didn't stop him. McTavish forced himself to his feet. The figure didn't seem interested in him. Instead, it continued hitting Ernest Lyle again and again, before it was suddenly blindsided by McTavish hitting it with his shoulder.

He'd gone down low, putting in as hard a tackle as he could. His body screamed at him. At his age, he shouldn't be throwing himself about. He did, however, bring the figure to the ground.

As McTavish went to hang on to the figure, he felt a punch to the head. His grip loosened, and he was pushed off to one side. His back hurt, but he'd get up again. Nobody did that.

As he got to his knees, he saw that the figure had stood up and was once again hitting Ernest Lyle. Lyle looked as if he would slip away into unconsciousness. He'd been covering himself up, but now the hands were limp.

Once again, McTavish raced towards the figure, but this time, it saw him coming and hit him with the back of its hand. McTavish fell backwards, hitting his head on the floor. It rang, and he struggled to get up. All he could see was the figure putting a few more blows onto Ernest Lyle, before it turned, ran to the front of the stage, and dropping the whip, jumped into the crowd.

There was chaos. People were screaming. Suddenly, the stage was full of security staff, but out in the crowd, most of which was in darkness, a surge went this way and that. There was screaming.

Angus went to get up, but arms were put around him. He looked up and saw Emma's face.

'You dear man,' she said. 'You dear man.'

She helped him sit upright and then wrapped herself around him. It was cold. He was aching, but he just stared out into the crowd. It looked like there were police running in from all angles, police and security staff. There were various Kampuses out there. That's what it was called, wasn't it? Kampus or a Krampus. There had been a few. Somebody had told him it was because of that blasted game, and he saw several were being tackled, but there were also other people panicking, running away.

\* \* \*

'What's the damage?' asked McTavish in the back of the ambulance.

'You've got off light. It's just a severe blow to the head. We're going to take you in for observation, just for the night.'

'Do you want me to come with you?' asked Emma. She was holding McTavish's hand. God bless the girl.

'No,' he said. 'I'm fine. I'm in expert hands. Besides, I'm old enough to be your grandfather. I can't have you sitting around with me. People will think it's creepy.'

*It would be creepy*, he thought, *and not good for the image, even if there was a part of him that wouldn't have minded her company*. She smiled and gave him a kiss on the cheek.

'I need to look at somebody else,' said the medic inside the ambulance. 'You wait here and then we'll get going. We might have a few others to transport with us. Don't get up.'

'I won't,' said McTavish. After the paramedic had left the vehicle, Angus said goodbye to Emma, hoping that the poor girl would be all right, for it had been a shock all round.

The stage manager entered the rear of the ambulance, giving a smile. 'You're okay then?'

'Bumps and bruises. What the hell was that about?'

'That guy, Ernest Lyle, he's not in a good way. The guy beat him hard. I reckon if he'd kept going, he might have whipped him to death. People are saying it's to do with the killings that have happened. It's chaos out there. Police have lifted a load of Krampuses. I think that's what it is, but who knows if they've got the right one? That costume was something else. There's been a stack of injuries as well, as people panicked. I'm telling you; this isn't good. Right in front of everyone, right in front of families, and everything.'

'You don't have to tell me. I was standing looking at it.'

'You did well though,' said the stage manager. If you hadn't tackled him like that, I don't know about that Ernest guy. Maybe he might not have made it. What have they said about the rest of the week?'

'They're just taking me in overnight for observation. I'll be fine to come back.'

'Up in the air at the moment.'

'It can't be. You can't let something like this stop it. This is Inverness. This is Christmas,' said Angus. 'We've got to get back up. We've got to go at it. We need to tell them.'

'I hear you. We'll have to see.'

'Police are going to have to allow it, aren't they?'

'They can hardly stop it. Anyway,' said the floor manager, 'you get better tonight and I'll talk to you in the morning. And well done. There might be a load of stuff in the paper about the horror of the attack, but your name will be right up there. You'll be a hero.'

Angus nodded. He didn't want to be a hero, just wanted people to have Christmas. He just wanted things to be normal. Not some idiot like this to cause such a problem. This was Inverness. He was proud of it. It was his city. It was where he was from, and they would not stop the city. He'd be back out there, sorting Christmas out.

# Chapter 13

'Can you believe it?' said Macleod. 'I think we've picked up every Krampus in the area that night and none of them match the guy who was on stage. How did he get away? How did he get out of that crowd?'

'Probably made the crowd split. I mean, having seen that on stage. I'd have run.'

Macleod glowered at Clarissa. 'No, you wouldn't have. You'd have taken him down.'

'Not anymore. I'd have let somebody else do it.'

'I've got everyone on me, the Chief Constable, press, the city's trade representatives, everyone, but we got lucky.' Macleod turned and looked across his office towards Hope.

'Lucky,' she said, 'Mr Lyle didn't feel very lucky.'

'Mr Lyle came away with his life, but it's definitely to do with the game. Sleigh bells and everything beforehand.'

'We should bring Maddie in,' said Hope. 'She's the one lead we've got. She is the one person who might lead us to what we want.'

'No,' said Clarissa, 'don't do it. The connection we've got isn't much. She's going to give up much more if she doesn't know you're looking. You bring her in, she'll shut down. If

111

she's meeting these other people, she will not do it once you've contacted her. Not in the sense of bringing her in, looking to arrest her. So far, everything you've done has been in the normal course of an investigation. She's not a suspect as far as she knows. Stay loose about it. Let me keep an eye on her.'

Hope looked across at Macleod.

'That's your call—your case, your call,' said Macleod. 'But if you want my opinion . . .' He saw Hope nod. 'Clarissa's right. Don't bring her in yet. I know we need results, but give it twenty-four hours.'

'We're going to have to do the press conference soon. Do we have anything else though?' asked Macleod.

'Ross has got his carrot he's chasing. There's definitely a different sort of carrot within the freezer. He's hoping he can trace a route through that.'

'We're looking at different protagonists, different killers,' said Clarissa. 'We're going to have to follow each one as best we can. The reason I'm saying we don't bring her in is because of when you look at the game,' said Clarissa. 'As far as I understand it, you're meant to prevent other people from not celebrating Christmas. Therefore, you have to be seen committing the murders. Be an example to the public.

'If Maddie did this first killing, it hasn't got out. Did she film it? Will it be going on social media? Hard to track her partners if she never puts it out. Will she meet with the rest? Do they compare? Who's done the best? Who's really brought the game to life? Because if they're playing the game in this fashion, THIS IS A GAME, isn't it?'

Macleod shook his shoulders. 'I don't know. I don't think we know at all.'

'Anyway,' said Clarissa, 'I better pick her up after leaving the shop.'

\* \* \*

It was the day after the beating of Ernest Lyle on the stage and the whole day had been chaos at the station. Ross was still seeking answers about who had picked up carrots of the variety he was looking into. And the entire investigation just felt as if it was waiting for something to break.

Clarissa donned her shawl and headed out into the city, taking up a position a little distance from the discount art shop. She clocked Maddie leaving it, and Clarissa followed her until Maddie went to her own home.

From there, she had dinner. Later, she departed on a bus to the edge of Inverness, and to an estate that was more than run down. Here, some houses were abandoned. There were very few people on the street.

Clarissa watched as Maddie entered an abandoned house. The brick structure was just about standing, but internally, the ceiling had collapsed. Maddie was picking through the rubble, moving several bricks, and then produced a bag. From that bag, she donned an elf outfit. She kept the scarf that she'd brought with her. Leaving the abandoned house, she walked down the street and round a few other corners until she found another one that seemed in even worse repair.

Clarissa crouched in the shadows, watching from a distance. There were rats sitting here and there, but inside there was a lone candle burning. Clarissa saw Maddie get up close to where the front door would've been. She said something that Clarissa couldn't hear, and then she stepped inside. Everywhere was frosty. Clarissa, having to be careful she didn't slip as she approached the building, crept forward, avoiding broken bricks. The top half of what had been a two-storey house seemed to have collapsed in. There was no roof.

As she approached one window, which still had glass in it, she peered through carefully. Looking inside, she pulled her shawl tight, for what she looked at gave her what she could only describe as the heebie-jeebies. Sitting in a circle was a Krampus, in the same outfit that had been seen the previous night. There was also a snowman. Santa was on the edge of the group too, and something with red eyes. It looked like what was the Badalisc; she wasn't so familiar with it, but maybe that's what it was supposed to be. And then the elf joined them.

Clarissa saw snow fall, and it was landing inside the house. It came down in a strong flurry, landing on the horns of the Krampus, but the five figures didn't move.

'He's not dead,' said Santa.

'But it was out in public. It was in front of everyone. That's what it's meant to be. Our elf friend didn't manage that. Our elf friend did it and nobody knows about it.'

'I did film it.'

'But nobody's seen it,' said the Krampus.

'It will be nothing to what I do.'

Clarissa thought this was coming from the Badalisc, but there was no part of the mask that was moved by the mouth, so the sound was probably coming from inside.

'Mine was filmed,' said the snowman. 'They just haven't let it out. Need to get that footage for it to be shown.'

'We're all players in the game,' said Santa. 'We know why we're doing this, because of the unfairness of it.'

As Clarissa listened to his voice, she found it intoxicating.

She noted that when he spoke, the others nodded. Time and again, he would suggest that things had to be more explicit. The killings they were carrying out had to be out in front so that people would know, because Christmas wasn't being celebrated. People were not being allowed to celebrate Christmas, and those that were, did not do it in the right way.

'Salute your efforts, Krampus, but you may have to revisit it. You didn't actually kill him, and he deserved to be killed.'

'I'll try, but it's hard.'

Clarissa looked down to her left and saw a couple of rats making their way across from her. She shivered inside. She really didn't like rats, really didn't like them. Clarissa looked back to where they were speaking again, although she couldn't hear that well.

The snow was now whipping down. While the circle of rather strange Christmas figures had some sort of shelter, she was hoping her shawl would keep her warm enough. She had gloves on as well, but inside she was getting cold.

Clarissa was struggling now to hear the lilting voice of Santa, having gone quieter, but she could see the other four were completely engaged by what he was saying. Maybe he was the ringleader. Either way, this was a time to get them, but she was on her own. She would need backup.

She couldn't risk making a call. Instead, taking her phone and making sure it was hidden behind the wall and not up near the window, she tapped out a message. She gave the address of where she was and asked for backup to come in quietly.

'Five suspects to arrest,' the message said. 'Tell Hope, tell Macleod.'

Clarissa would have to wait. Any chance of alerting the figures beforehand was a bad idea and they could leave, flee.

Should only take ten minutes for her colleagues to arrive. After all, they were still in Inverness.

And then she saw Santa stand. The others stood with him. If they were going to leave, should Clarissa tail them? She would know where Maddie was. They knew where the girl lived. But the others, did she stick to one of them? Maybe Santa, for he seemed like the ringleader. She would need to get across though. Her current position would be seen by all when they exited. Carefully, she walked over, racing through the gap in the house where they'd entered. As she did so, her foot disturbed a rat and suddenly Clarissa felt something bite her leg. She tumbled to the ground across brickwork and let out a yelp.

'Who's that?' said Santa.

'Get out of here. We need to get out of here.' It sounded like the Krampus. Suddenly, everyone was running. 'Bugger it,' said Clarissa, hauling herself up, but finding that a rat was still biting into her leg. Summoning up every bit of courage she had, she grasped it around the neck, picked it up and flung it as hard as she could. It hit the snowman running out of the door. He shouted, but then disappeared off in the swirling snow.

Clarissa got up on her feet, though, and as Maddie took off, she ran over. The girl stopped, turned the other way, and Clarissa ran round the outside of the building. Through the window, she could see Maddie was making her way over to the far side of the house where the wall had fallen down.

Clarissa ran as hard as she could, puffing, and realised she would not make it. She stopped, picked up some bricks, and started lobbing them towards that exit. Maddie stopped in her elf outfit, turned, ran the other way, back out where she originally had tried to escape from, surmising that Clarissa must be at the other exit. Clarissa turned back, and this time had a short enough distance to be there first.

As Maddie exploded through the exit, Clarissa stuck her foot out. Maddie tripped, slid forward, and smacked her head off a small remnant of wall before collapsing on the ground. Clarissa reached down, pulled the woman's arms behind her and slapped on the handcuffs before turning to look for the rest. In the swirling snow, there was no one. They had all fled. She was left with the one person who had already committed her murder.

There were no sirens as the police cars arrived, but when they did, they found Clarissa standing over a prone elf on the ground with its hands cuffed behind its back.

'Who's that? Is that her?' said Hope, marching forward. The woman was in jeans, T-shirt and leather jacket, while Clarissa stood freezing, rubbing her arms.

'They were all here. All here. I got bit by a bloody rat.'

'We had them all. We could have stopped this,' said Hope. 'We had them all.'

Macleod appeared from behind Hope and knelt down, looking at Clarissa's leg. 'You need to get to the hospital. You'll need a tetanus jab on that. Go do that. Get sorted. Then come back, Okay?'

'Tell me about them,' said Hope to Clarissa.

'They're gone, Hope,' said Macleod. 'Let's get her sorted in case that gets infected. Then she'll come back. You've got a long night ahead of you. That's your girl in the elf outfit. It's time to ask some questions.'

Hope watched as Clarissa was taken away to one of the police cars to head for the hospital.

'We could have had them, Seoras. We could have had them

all.'

'Clarissa was exposed on her own out in the open,' said Macleod.

'She didn't have to react to them, though.'

'No, but she didn't. She called it in,' said Macleod. 'And she got bitten by a rat.'

'But we're back with nothing. She's committed her murder, that girl.'

'We haven't got nothing. Theory's right; everything fits. Five of them, five costumes. You've got one, another one's already committed their murder, so we've got time with that one. Three to get. You'll need to debrief Clarissa, and then sort out Maddie. Still, at least we've got something we can tell the press.'

Hope looked at him. 'You want me to stand up in front of the press and tell them that we busted up a conference between Frosty the Snowman, two foreign festive figures, an elf and Santa Claus?'

'Well, it's the truth,' said Macleod. Hope stared at him. 'Ho, ho, ho,' said Macleod and turned back to the car.

# Chapter 14

Early the next morning, the team was gathered together. Hope called the meeting after the previous night's excitement with Clarissa. Clarissa had been to the hospital, taken a tetanus jab and had her wound patched up. Hope smiled at her as the woman arrived early that morning for work. The arrest happened at night. During the time their suspect had gone through processing, Hope decided she wanted a fresh approach first thing in the morning.

Hope would do the interviewing, but she also wanted to run through with everyone where they were at. This was as much to focus her own mind on what she was trying to get out of Maddie in the next few hours. She also needed some information on Ernest Lyle and had sent Cunningham off to investigate. Now everyone was pooled together within her office around the small round table. Macleod had come down as well.

'Morning, everyone,' said Hope as the team looked back at her. 'I just wanted to check in and see where we were all going this morning. I'm going to be tied up for most of it, probably with Seoras talking to Maddie Jefferson about her part in all of this. She's been wearing the outfit of an elf and meeting with the others. Clarissa has identified the Krampus outfit at this meeting as being the same as the one worn on stage during the attack. First off, Susan, Mr Lyle's employees—who are they, and have they got any suspects amongst them?'

'Not really,' said Susan Cunningham. She was dressed in blue jeans and a T-shirt as if summer had never gone away. Macleod thought she was like a mini-Hope.

'Thing is, he only has his family working for him,' she said. 'They were all there when the Krampus attacked, so it wasn't any of them in the outfit. Other than that, he's got no employees, so I'm not sure why he's not seen as a great celebrant of Christmas.'

'Well, that's something we're going to have to look into,' said Hope.

'Do you want me to announce the arrest?' asked Macleod. 'I'm more than happy to. It's going to look good with the press and probably help with the public, but I'll hold off if necessary.'

'Hold off,' said Hope. 'Don't make it public knowledge if you're asked if anyone's in with us. Just say there's someone being held with our inquiries. Don't say who it is. We'll charge her soon enough.'

'Susan, this morning,' said Hope, 'I want you back to the scene of last night's meeting. See what else can be learned and see if we can search for where others may have hidden their costumes. They may have moved them, but we may find out something where they've stored them before. Clarissa said that Maddie's was close to the meeting.'

'That's correct. I can't see them walking around before their meetings. She was only around the corner and in a derelict house.'

'They may have defaulted to their previous actions,' said

Hope, 'in that they may have just stored them quickly while they were escaping. On the other hand, they may have run off properly and may still have the items with them. In which case, we need to be on the lookout for them, too. Jona's team will have gone over everything. See if they've picked anything up, Susan. I believe you're off somewhere, Ross.'

'I've found some details of carrot seeds sold in the Inverness area and I've got a woman's address in Drumnadrochit,' said Ross. 'I'm going there direct from here.'

'And you're hoping to find?' asked Clarissa.

'Someone has bought these carrots. In which case, if the carrot has come from there, I see if they've had any stolen. I see if they've used them; see what sort of crop they had. It's a long shot, but it's a shot. We do have an unexplained carrot, or rather, a variety of carrot in the freezer where Sadiq Muhammad was murdered. I'll also bring it back to see if we can get a better match. Show that the carrot actually came from that strain. At the moment, we don't have a link to who our snowman is, and we also don't have a snowman who needs to kill again. This may be a way of linking him in.'

'Good,' said Hope. 'Now, that's everything.'

'No,' said Clarissa. 'Just everybody be advised. These people sat down and played this like a game, except for one. Whenever the Santa Claus spoke, everyone was engaged in him, totally. I don't know if it's a father-figure type idea. I don't know if it's the fact that he has a way of talking, a way of manipulating, but they were certainly looking to him.

'He also talked about the idea of the game being public when you kill people, that other people must learn from it. Our snowman may try to highlight what he's done. He said he was recorded on CCTV, but the Santa Claus gave the impression that it wasn't public enough. Our Krampus was very public, but didn't actually kill their victim. This was brought up.'

'The other thing to remember,' said Macleod, 'is that we only have a few days till Christmas, less than a week. If they're going to do this, it's going to be pre-Christmas Day, or possibly on Christmas Day. Once you get beyond that, what's the point? Expect something to happen soon.'

'On that dour note,' said Hope, 'let's go.'

Macleod went downstairs with Hope to interview Maddie Jefferson. She was sitting across the table, no longer in her elf outfit but in basic loaned clothing, her own garments having been taken away for forensic analysis.

'Maddie, you were wearing an elf outfit last night, discussing murder with several other people. We have had a case already of someone being murdered within a department store in the changing rooms. We're not sure what they were dressed as.'

'That was me,' said Maddie. 'I was dressed as an elf.'

'You're confessing to the murder?' asked Hope.

'Absolutely.'

'Would you like to explain how you did it?'

Maddie shuffled in her seat for a moment and then grinned.

'Well, I came in through the department entrance to the changing rooms. That's the rear entrance. It's sort of the corridor for colleagues. A friend of mine used to work there and told me about it. When I came in, I waited until the girl running the changing rooms went on break. There was nobody to cover. I knew that because it's been like that for the last couple of weeks.

'I saw Greenwood trying some outfits. As soon as I saw her pick them up, that's when I went round the back and in. I was fortunate enough that there wasn't anybody else in, so I changed into my costume, and I went at her with a knife. A large butcher's-type knife, which I bought several weeks ago. I would have done the killing earlier, but she was awkward to tie down. I looked at home and things like that, but it wasn't public enough. Maybe it wasn't public enough either, what I did.'

'Not public enough?'

'I hoped that somebody would actually come in while I was dressed up as the elf. There was a lot of blood everywhere, but I couldn't wait around forever. Washing the outfit was a nightmare. Once I'd killed her, I got in a bit of a panic because I needed to get to that exit. While I had a knife in my hand, I guessed I thought I could charge at people and they'd run away, and then I could go out the rear exit. But that sort of idea became less and less appealing, and in the end, I went to the exit, got changed, and walked out with the costume in the bag. I cleaned it at my house . . . was able to wear it again then when we had meetings.'

Hope stood up from her chair, not quite believing how open the girl was being.

'Who's the other lot, then?'

'That's the other gamers. I think it's a game, isn't it?'

'There is a game being played,' said Hope. 'I take it you're referring to *Winter Slay Bells*.'

'That's the one. It's a brilliant game,' said Maddie. 'We're just playing it in real life. I mean, the idea is right, isn't it? Some people are miserable. Alice Greenwood, she was miserable.'

'How did you meet them?' asked Hope.

'In a game forum. We were discussing the game, and we all were a little pissed off. I think that's the best way to describe it.'

'Pissed off?' said Macleod. 'You've killed someone because you were pissed off.'

'I didn't really think about it like that,' said Maddie. The girl was still smiling. 'We got together. We didn't know who anybody was because on the game forum, we all used cryptic descriptions and that.'

'What game forum?' asked Macleod.

'Oh no, I'm not telling you that. That would give the game away. I'm quite happy to tell you what we do.'

*She wants the notoriety,* thought Hope. *They want everything to be held up, but they don't want to be caught unless, well, unless they've already done what they need to do. She thinks she's going to be applauded for this.*

'You said you were all pissed off,' said Hope. 'In what way?'

Maddie went forward on the table, elbows touching it, and looked across at Hope. 'Alice Greenwood took a day off in the run-up to Christmas. I wasn't allowed any. We didn't have enough staff. She took a whole day off. People like that, killing Christmas time. We all need to celebrate, but it isn't about that anymore, is it? It's all about this machine, this money, money, money. Buy this, buy that, and plebs like me are the ones that must sit and work while you buy.

'What do I get? Christmas Eve at a ridiculous time of night. You aren't even ready. You haven't got anything done. I am not allowed any time off in December. How is that fair?'

Hope saw the girl stare at Macleod, almost begging him for an answer. She had killed someone, and she was standing there trying to defend her rights. It was almost surreal.

'Did the rest of them have employers that did this?' asked Macleod.

'No, not all. Not in the same way. We all have our own thing.'

124

'The other night, when my colleague saw you before she caught you, you were all discussing. Do you meet there often?'

'We'll not be meeting there anymore, will we?' laughed Maddie. 'When we decided we were going to do something about all being pissed off,'—She said the word as if it was good to annoy Macleod, who looked uncomfortable with it—'that's when we decided we would meet, but we said we couldn't know who each other was. It was fine on the game forum because you never got to see who each other was. Even if you put yourself on a screen, you could mask who you were.

'When we said, "Shall we do something about it?" Santa took the lead. Santa was the one who organised the house, so we'd meet there. He got me to order the costumes, told me how to do it with cash, and never actually meet our costume designer. I got all the sizes and sent them in.

'We then dropped the costumes at certain places. Never went back to those places. Once you picked up your costume, it was up to you to hide it, but you were hiding it within the locale of where we were going to for our meetings. All worked really well. We got to meet, and Santa took the lead. We had to have some rules about how the game was going to be played. At the end of the day, it's not just a game anymore, is it? It's actually showing people what that game does.

'This is the thing,' said Maddie suddenly, and she almost looked like she was preaching. 'Christmas has been ruined. That game had the right idea. People will say that it was just a game. It's fun, but it had the right idea. People needed to be taught the importance of Christmas, the importance of people having time. I don't mean religiously. We're not religious nuts. I mean, none of us are Christian, I think.'

*Really?* thought Hope. *You surprise me.*

'Thing is,' said Maddie, 'we're going to have an effect. The Krampus the other night, he'll have an effect. People won't go out and buy. We need to break this stupid cycle of just buying, buying, and spending at Christmas. It needs to go back to be about family, about having time with friends, having a time to enjoy ourselves. That's what the Winter Festival was meant to be about, or having time to be with your God, if that's what you do. I mean, I've nothing against God.'

'Just people who shop,' said Macleod. 'How long have you been operating at that abandoned house?'

'A month. We were getting ourselves up and ready.'

Hope knelt down and whispered in Macleod's ear, 'I'll be a moment,' and then she disappeared out of the interview room. She grabbed a nearby constable and sent instructions to the team to collect things from Maddie's house. After getting a search warrant, anything electrical, and to get Ross onto it, see if they could work out which game forum it was. Maybe they could identify the players. Hope had little faith in that, though, for Maddie was giving it up far too easily. She returned to the room.

'I'm glad you're here. He's a bundle of laughs, him.' Maddie smirked at Macleod.

'Maddie,' said Hope, 'would you say the game has to be played out before Christmas?'

'Christmas Day at the latest,' said Maddie. 'That's what we agreed. After all, what's the point of telling people to celebrate Christmas properly after it's been and gone? You're stuffed until next year.'

'You're obviously quite happy about being caught. Why is that?'

'I'm not happy, but you'll tell people you've brought someone in. It gets exposure. That's what we were told. That's the key thing. Exposure.' She looked down at the table.

'Who told you that?' asked Macleod.

'Father Christmas,' said Maddie. 'He's going to bring one heck of a sack of presents this Christmas.'

The woman leant back in her chair and laughed repeatedly. Hope wondered if she was stable. She brutally murdered someone, and yet she seemed to have neither remorse nor trauma from it. Hope took Macleod outside. She needed a coffee, and she needed to regroup, to think about what else she could learn from Maddie.

# Chapter 15

Ross drove along the side of Loch Ness, enjoying the early morning view on his way to Drumnadrochit. The address he was looking for was a smallish house located just outside the village. He saw it had a few fields with a couple of animals in them. As he pulled the car up, he saw a woman with a wheelbarrow walking around the side of the house. She was grey of hair, quite bony, but for all that, seemed reasonably fit.

There was snow on the ground. Following the previous busy night, Ross hadn't yet got round to changing his shoes for boots. Their black leather seemed to disappear into the snow and he felt chilled in his suit. However, he shouted from the car to make sure he was in the right place.

'Hello, would you be Marion Barnes?' he asked loudly.

The woman stopped, put down the wheelbarrow, and turned to face him. Her face was almost hawkish, very definite lines with the skin drawn tight. However, there were wrinkles here and there beyond the cheekbones and where the jaw jutted out. She would be described as an interesting woman if not beautiful, and her eyes peered intently towards Ross.

'Who's asking?'

'I'm Detective Constable Alan Ross,' he said. 'I'm seeking information on some carrots you bought.'

'You got some ID, son?' asked the woman.

Ross reached inside his jacket and held up his warrant card. The woman walked slowly up towards the gate and then took the warrant card off Ross, staring at it. After a moment, she reached inside her jacket, took out a pair of spectacles, putting them on, and spent the next two minutes scanning the warrant card. Then she handed it back to him.

'Constable, not important then. Just a grunt.'

'I don't know if you're important,' said Ross. 'Do you grow carrots?'

'I grow a lot of things,' said the woman, 'including carrots. My name is Marion Barnes. You got that right.'

'Do you mind if I come in and ask you some questions?'

'Come with me. I'm just going out to the greenhouses. Got some things to pick. You can give me a hand.'

Ross would rather have gone inside, but he couldn't very well insist on it. This woman might have been awkward. He shut the car door, locked it, and opened the gate.

'You can pick up the wheelbarrow and follow me.'

*I can, can I?* thought Ross. *Cheers.* When they rounded the house, Ross saw at least six greenhouses behind it. She had a reasonable bit of land.

'Do you sell this stuff or is this a sort of project?'

'I'm retired, and I eat it. I keep it for me, most of it. A few neighbours get bits and pieces; they give me bits and pieces back. Gives me something to do, keeps me going. Otherwise, I'd sit in a chair in there and rot, and that doesn't do anybody any good, does it?'

'No, I'm sure it doesn't,' said Ross.

'You said about carrots. Carrots are over there in that greenhouse.'

'I'm looking for a specific type of carrot. '

'Well, I've got lots of carrots. I grow lots of old varieties. Same with broccoli, and the cauliflower. You probably don't recognise a cauliflower, do you? Because it's not white. Nowadays all the supermarkets, it's white cauliflower. That's the only type. Cauliflower came in all sorts; so did carrots.

'Potatoes? People don't like purple potatoes, do they? Many bits and bobs we used to do. You grew what grew, at what time of year it grew. Nowadays, you force everything. You do this and that, but it's good for you. Good for you to grow your own. Lots of different colours—that's what they tell you. They use all those colours in that rainbow for those gender people these days, don't they? Colours were all about health when I was growing up. In school, eat all the different colours is what they said, and we had lots of different colours then.'

'Excellent,' said Ross, almost absentmindedly. 'I'm looking for a St. Valery.'

The old woman stopped for a moment, turning to Ross. 'St. Valery? Know your carrots then, do you?'

'Not really,' said Ross. He followed her into a small greenhouse. It had a lot of green leaves coming out of beds.

'You'd recognise these as carrot leaves, wouldn't you?' She said to him, but Ross would recognise them as nothing of the sort. 'If you say so,' he said.

'Can you see the St. Valery?' she said. Ross could see carrots that had been pulled out sitting in a small wooden basket. There were white ones, yellow ones, there were some purple ones, and there were some orange ones.

'It's going to be one of the orange ones,' he said.

'It's the only orange one. I only grow St. Valery orange ones and that's because they're so old. Some of the neighbours don't like it if you give away the other colours. Don't see them as carrots. "Oh, is that a parsnip?" No, it's a carrot,' said the woman derogatorily. 'Some of them couldn't tell their arse from their elbow when it comes to food.'

'Do you know anybody else that grows it, locally?' asked Ross.

'No, said the woman, 'I don't. Here,' she handed him a trowel, 'dig a few up from there. Don't rip the leaves off the top. We'll sort that out later.'

Ross dug down and, to his surprise, pulled out a purple carrot.

'Do you want a couple to take home with you?'

'I'm afraid I can't,' said Ross. 'It would be good,' he lied, 'but because I'm asking you questions and what it's tied to, I need to not take anything from you.'

The woman froze for a moment, then stared at him. 'What are you investigating? These are carrots.'

'I have to inform you I'm investigating a murder and a carrot of this type may have been used.'

The woman burst out laughing. 'How do you kill someone with a carrot? They're not that pointy, you can't sharpen them. It don't work like that, killing people with carrots. You're insane.'

'No,' said Ross, 'I'm afraid you don't understand. There was a costume worn by the killer, and part of that costume was a carrot, and it was a St. Valery carrot. It's broken off and gone into a freezer. I need to know where the St. Valery carrots are grown in this area. You're the only one I've found so far.'

'That makes me the bloody killer. I think you're way ahead

131

of yourself there.'

'No, it doesn't make you the killer. Perhaps you knew the killer,' said Ross, 'but it makes me wonder if they got the carrots from you. I need to know who's taking your St Valery's.'

'No one yet,' she said.

'Do you have any family?' asked Ross.

'No, I don't,' she said. 'Never had kids. I've got nephews and nieces somewhere, but they don't come to visit. Not that it bothers me. I'm quite happy.'

'You have given none of your St Valery's away?'

'No,' she said, 'I don't think so. Not yet. Given some of the purple ones away and some of the yellow ones. We did that. I remember that, but I think those have just been here. They've not gone away from me. I ate a few the other day. Anyway, get some of the rest of them up and we'll take them inside. You must be frozen wearing a suit out here. It's snowing. You don't realise it's snowing?'

Ross raised his eyebrows, but he didn't take the bait. Instead, he dug up some carrots and put them out into the basket before following the lady inside with it.

'Go into the front room,' said the woman, 'I'll make you a cup of tea.'

'I don't mind,' said Ross, but the woman insisted. Pushing him on in, Ross found a large stove inside, which was burning wooden logs. He stood in front of it and then turned round so his bottom was facing it, warming his hands behind him. He looked around, but there weren't many photos. There was the occasional one of an animal, some vegetables that had been grown, some places that the woman maybe had been. There was one photograph of her with a young lad.

'Detective Constable, you take your tea black. That's the way

I take it.'

Ross didn't take tea at all, but whatever.

'I got the Valery's from a website. I'm not a total ignoramus, Even I know how to use a website. I used to live down in England. They did a lot more varieties down there. I try to get some Scottish ones when I'm up here, but I like St Valery's. Nice flavour off them. You ever eaten any?'

'No,' said Ross.

'Then you should take some.'

'I told you I can't. Can I ask you a question, though?'

'You're a detective, aren't you?' she said. 'Guess that's what you're going to do.'

'Just a boy in the photograph.'

'Oh, him. John. John comes every, what is it, fortnight, a week. He was a bit of a bad lad. Nicked something or whatever, so he comes as community service. I don't need the help, I can run this place, but I get somebody like him off his arse and doing stuff instead of languishing in a jail or whatever. Somewhere like that. "Community service," the judge said. Isle of Man had it right, hit them with the birch, but no, that's not what we do here. Would you do that? You think it's better to hit them with the birch?'

Ross froze for a minute. *Birch. The Krampus had hit somebody with a birch. Did she just say it by accident?*

'Do you have any birch?' asked Ross.

'No,' laughed the woman, 'I don't. Besides, I couldn't swing anything.'

Ross looked at her. Yes, she couldn't have picked up anyone. To run in quickly to a store, pick someone up and fight with them and to put them inside a freezer. It wasn't happening. This wasn't the person who was inside the snowman's costume, that was for sure.

'What's John's name? What's his second name?' asked Ross.

'Parish. Told you, he comes and does community service.'

'So, he's your helper, so he knows about all the stuff around here, does he?'

'Well, he's learning. I was telling him about different things. He's been less than attentive. I don't think he's that clever, to be honest. Did it as a community thing. I just wanted to help. I'm all for giving these kids a good chance, a better start. Just because you do something wrong doesn't mean you're a bad egg for life, does it?'

'No,' said Ross, 'it doesn't. Has he ever shown any interest in your carrots?'

'Carrots,' said the woman suddenly, 'you were talking about the carrots. St Valery, you ever eaten them?'

*She's slightly behind the drag curve on a few things*, thought Ross, and he wondered just how much of what she was saying was accurate.

'I was asking you about John Parish. Has he ever taken any interest in the carrots?'

'Doesn't take any interest in any of the vegetables. He's best slopping out some animals. He don't talk that much, either. Comes along, does it, because he has to. Go and be with the daft old biddy, that's what he'll be thinking. He's not stupid enough to steal from me or do anything like that either, though. Because I'd report him and then he'd get more stuff dumped on him. Told him that when he came through that door. I told him. I said, "I'll give you a decent report, but one, don't piss me off; two, don't steal from me; and three, don't wind me up. You're here to help, so get your finger out of your arse and get on with it."'

Ross found the woman hilarious but was doing his best not to laugh. 'So, he hasn't gone near any of the carrots,' he said.

'The St. Valerys. He wanted a St. Valery—well, he didn't actually want a St. Valery—he wanted an orange carrot,' said Marion, 'and I gave him one. Which would be the St. Valery, as I don't have any other orange carrots.'

'One,' said Ross. 'just the one. Was he not hungry?'

'No, not that. He only wanted one, and it had to be orange. I was going to give him some of the white ones or the purple ones. He said, 'You can't do that.'

'Why?' asked Ross.

'I don't know. He was asking me for a carrot. I wasn't that bothered. I had things to do. Besides, he needed to clean out the animals. That's where he's good. I can't shovel shit all day,' she said. 'Animals, it's animals you've got to look after, and you've got to clean the place.'

'Just a moment,' said Ross. 'What did he take?'

'He took a carrot.'

'Which one? Clarify it for me,' said Ross. 'Which one?'

'One of the St. Valerys.'

'He only wanted one,' said Ross.

'Yes. Do you not have a notebook or something,' she said, 'something to write this down in, because you seem to ask me the same questions repeatedly.' Ross ignored her and made a mental note of everything that was being said.

'I'm going to need to take one of your St. Valery carrots with me,' said Ross, 'if that's okay with you.'

'You said you couldn't take anything from me.'

'This is regarding the investigation,' said Ross. 'When's John Parrish due here again?'

'Not for a couple of weeks. It'll be after Christmas now,' said

135

Marion.

'Okay. Can I take one of your carrots then?'

Fifteen minutes later, Ross was back in the car, carrot beside him on the seat. He turned the heating in the car up because of the coldness, but inside there was an excitement forming. He was getting close. This may be something.

He pulled away onto the roads which had been cleared and looked at the snowbanks at the side of the road as he drove past. The other side of Loch Ness was a mix of green and white. A part of him felt Christmas was in full swing. He still had to get presents for his partner, Angus, and their boy. Maybe if he could get this piece of evidence over to Jona, and seize Parrish, just maybe, he could get this wrapped up early. Then he'd get a couple of days to actually enjoy the festive season.

# Chapter 16

Alan Ross parked up in the car park at the rear of the Inverness Police Station, then stepped out into the sludgy deposits of snow. Elsewhere, the snow hadn't melted like this, but elsewhere, cars hadn't been over it several times. He picked up the edges of his trousers, keen not to get them wet as he crossed to the steps and the rear entrance.

*Snow was lovely,* he thought, *in some ways. Beautiful on a picture postcard. Great even to see kids playing in it. There was also the other side when it got destroyed. Cars drove over it. When it melted, it went slushy.*

Alan was a snappy dresser in his own way and he hated his clothing getting soaked through. It would be dirty snow as well. He looked at his shoes as he shook them off inside the rear entrance. A bit of the snow had got up and over his right shoe and his ankle was feeling chilled. Still, there were more important things to worry about.

He climbed the stairs up to the office and as soon as he walked through the door, he heard the shout from the smaller interior office of his boss, Hope McGrath.

'Alan, don't move.'

Alan ignored the instruction and walked over to hang his

suit jacket up on the clothing pegs. From there he wandered and sat down behind his desk, looking at the various bits of paper all over it. Beside him, a constable went to speak, but as Alan looked up, a tall red-headed figure was looking down.

'No, I've got him first. Ross, we need you. We've got the computers of Maddie Jefferson coming back. All her tablets, phones, whatever. I need you to get on to it. I need you to find out what's inside of it.'

'All of it?' asked Ross. 'You know I'm going through the witness statements.'

'Get Patterson to take care of that. I need you for this.'

'But I've got something else,' said Ross.

'What?' asked Hope impatiently.

'The carrots. The carrots have come up trumps.'

'In what way?'

Ross told his tale of meeting Marion Burns and the St. Valery carrot, and of how he believed she was the only one growing them in the local area. A single carrot had been taken by John Parrish, a community service regular of Marion.

'So, you see,' said Ross, 'this could be him. He could be the snowman. He could be Frosty.'

Beside them, a constable turned. 'I wish we wouldn't call them Frosty the Snowman or the elf, the happy elf. Give them names. These are not nice. It's easier to think of them just as dress-up characters. Not real.'

Hope turned her head sideways, staring at the constable. 'One, they're not real, and two, I'm in conversation.'

The constable put her head down. Alan could see that Hope was in one of her more forceful moods. She was never nasty with people. Hope was always the reasonable one. Macleod was the one who could snap and push on through, especially when he was hyper fixated on something. Not Hope.

Yet she was learning to extract a bit of fear from those around her. Not that they wouldn't come to her. They had a respect that what she said went. Ross had worked with her for too long to require that sort of fear. He understood. She never asked for stuff unless she was certain that it was more important than what you were doing. However, Ross wasn't so sure this time.

'I can't follow that up if I'm doing all the computer work.'

Hope stood up to her full height, and spun round, scanning around the room. 'Clarissa, over here, please.'

Clarissa walked over. Not quickly. For she never took instruction joyfully—such was her nature. She arrived in reasonable time. Hope had Ross explain to Clarissa all about the St. Valery carrot.

'This is Ross's. He should take this.'

'Ross has got more important things to do. He's got to go through all the computers of Maddie Jefferson. We may be able to trace everybody from there. If we can find those emails, if we can find the contacts, we might trace the others.'

'I get to hunt carrots,' said Clarissa. 'When I came back to help, I thought coming off my holiday, oh, they'll put you right at the top here. You'll be bang in the middle of this one, Clarissa. I know I'm halfway out the door, but there's no need to send me on a carrot hunt to prove it.'

Clarissa strode off. Hope gave her a worried look, but turned, shaking her shoulders at Ross.

'She's not being serious. She's just winding you up,' said Ross.

Hope shook her head. Ross thought it was the last thing she needed. The stress was telling. He couldn't blame her.

139

After all, this was Christmas time. If there were deaths in the city, deaths associated with retail, all hell would break loose. Shopkeepers, trade associations, the public, the press.

That was the joy of doing his job. He didn't have to deal with the press very often. As the expert in surveillance and computers, he was very much pigeon'd into what he did. Running an investigation, keeping sure all the bits and pieces were kept in line, but he'd enjoyed himself going out there these days. He'd always did. If he moved up to sergeant, that's what he'd be doing more of.

Ross wondered if he wanted it or not. As was his way, he put the question off for later, and thought about how to get hold of the computer material and the best way to hack in.

Hope, in the meantime, had returned to her office, where Susan Cunningham sat with Macleod. Hope slid round behind her desk, but then watched Susan stand up and move across to the whiteboard on the wall.

'If we're going to find this group, other than with electronic means, then we're going to have to go through their victims. At the moment, we don't know that many of them. Three out of five, two of which are dead. Of those who killed them, one's at large, and one's already sitting downstairs. Mr Lyle, on the other hand, is very much alive. Very much, I think, at risk.'

'In the game,' said Macleod, 'these people are accused of not having Christmas cheer. Not celebrating it correctly. Then, as you do, you go off and kill them in front of people. Murder them to make your point. That's been done here, but they haven't done it so successfully. They've been a little more worried about being so demonstratively obvious.'

'Or they just haven't got it,' said Susan.

'What do you mean?' asked Hope.

'Maddie went to kill Alice Greenwood in the changing room. She thought there'd be more people there. She waited until it was quiet so she could physically attack her. Then she thought there'd be people, racing in, people there to witness all the blood. She thought she'd be making a rather good statement.

'CCTV for the second one. Frosty the Snowman marches in. He knows he's on CCTV, so he dumps Sadiq into the freezer. He thinks they're going to play all the footage of it on TV. I mean, seriously, they're not that clever, are they? But the Ernest Lyle one, oh, the Krampus comes right up on stage in front of everyone. He's got it. He knows what has to be done, he just hasn't got a weapon that finishes it quick enough. If old McTavish hadn't pitched in, he might've done it. That's actual terror, that's real notoriety, and I think that's what the next two will go for.'

'We've got two of them still out there. Would they double up? Would the snowman come back and do another one?' asked Macleod.

'What you're saying,' said Hope, standing up from a chair and walking over to Susan, 'is that we need to find people with a grudge about Christmas against Lyle. What does Lyle do? Sadiq, he decides whether people can have time off. That's a similar line as Maddie, but that's not the case with Lyle. Lyle's family work for him. Unless the family are doing it, which they can't be, because they were in the crowd.'

'Exactly,' said Susan.

'We've got to find somebody else who's got something against Lyle. We need to understand all of this, but to understand it, the only thing we've got is Maddie downstairs,' said Macleod, 'who's not telling us an awful lot other than she did it and anything about what she did, because she knows

141

she's caught. She's not giving up anything about anyone else.'

'Maybe she did,' said Hope, 'all the communication is on these group chats they had. Potentially emails.'

'Except for when they met in person. Did she make notes about their meetings?' asked Cunningham. 'She will not tell you about them. She's not going to dob on them. And frankly, she doesn't seem so worried about her computers being lifted. What if she's got notes hidden away?'

'I mean, it's an awful lot to go to these meetings and just keep everything in your head. At some point, she'd have written sizes down for getting all the costumes done. What's everybody else organising? Why did that all just get dumped on Maddie? Were the group doing other things? Were there other parts to what they're about? She talked about walking into the back of the changing rooms. A friend told her that. A friend told her how to get into the back and through to the changing rooms. Did they, or was it the other who went and researched this?'

'You could,' said Susan, 'plan each other's murders. Then you wouldn't be seen beforehand. You wouldn't be there. Maddie was there at the store only on the day. We haven't seen her before.'

Macleod raised his hand up, rubbing his chin. 'You're right,' he said. 'It's too much to expect everything done simply on laptops or computers, and you'd also be worried if they get lifted. The best thing to have is a pen and paper. Write it down and then burn it. But if you're not finished with it, you might store it somewhere.'

He turned and looked at Hope.

'Well, I don't see any other lines of attack. Ross is already covering off the computers and Clarissa's chasing carrots.'

Macleod raised an eyebrow, but Hope put her hand up to show she didn't want to field that question just now.

'Susan, go down to Maddie Jefferson's house. Search it. Search it properly, thoroughly. See if there's anything under floorboards, under beds, anywhere she could store notes. Organise it with uniform.'

'The other thing . . .' said Macleod.

'Is we're going to need a watch on Lyle,' said Hope. 'A proper watch.'

'Exactly,' said Macleod. 'I'd do it, except it's growing arms and legs, the media side. I know you would normally take that, but I'm going to have to take it. They're wanting a more senior level.'

'We'll get Uniform to monitor him,' said Hope. 'I can't afford people out of here. We need detectives detecting out there. Uniform can protect.'

'Very good,' said Macleod. He watched as Susan Cunningham departed the room and then saw Hope return behind her desk. She dropped her elbows on the table and planted her face firmly into her hands, covering up her eyes.

'Seriously, Seoras? Christmas and we get figures running around killing people. I mean, Frosty the Snowman; we got Santa coming up; the elf. Do people not think about kids? Surely, they must think about kids with all of this.'

'You're doing everything,' said Macleod. 'Don't go into this. Don't start looking beyond your murderers. Don't start talking about what they're doing to anyone else. We have one task, find them and stop them. That's all. We do that and nobody else cares about us. We're judged on this one thing. Stopping them making the next murder. I think you're covering off all the right things, Hope.'

'What's your mate say?'

Macleod looked over to the corner of the room. A man stood in the grey habit, the hood covering the face, obscuring it from Macleod's sight. 'Next one's dead soon,' said a voice in Macleod's head.

'He's not very hopeful,' said Macleod, 'but he's been wrong before. He'll be wrong again.'

Macleod stood up and went to walk out of the room, but Hope stopped him. 'Seoras, how do you do that? How do you just dismiss this guy over there, this person you're seeing? How do you, in the middle of all of that, carry on?'

'It's more fun at the press conference,' said Macleod. 'Sometimes he's beside that guy from the courier—you know, the really annoying one?'

'Donaldson. He's beside Donaldson.'

'Yes, and he's saying to me, you're messing this up, you're doing this wrong, Seoras, all this stuff. I say to him, "Can't you just turn around and get rid of that guy?"'

Hope burst out laughing. 'That's ridiculous. You can't tell him that.'

'Why not?' said Macleod. 'He's not real. He will not turn around and actually kill him. Remember, this isn't an elf or Frosty the Snowman killing these people. It's just people killing people. It's what we always deal with. We've got to put aside the shock value that they're putting to it and get back to why they're doing it.

'Very few people just kill people for the fun of it. Computer games have been around for a long time. Not that many of them have ever made people go out and kill anyone else. *Winter Slay Bells* isn't doing that. It's a ridiculous game. Most of the people that play it think it's ridiculous. It's escapism. A world where they can do what they want. They know you can't do it in this world. We're hunting people that don't know that ever!

'The idea that someone doesn't celebrate Christmas or allow you to celebrate it the way you want and you feel the need to destroy them. That's a very dark thought,' said Macleod. 'But the thought that you gather in a group and dress up to do it, that's one of two things. Lunacy, which I don't think is at play here or a deliberately planned action, distracting people, terrorising them. This is about more than just the people being killed.

'We're looking for people who want to impose their will upon others. Possibly just to shock them and terrify them. I saw Maddie Jefferson. She didn't seem to be quite that type of person. Impressionable, yes. There'll be a ringleader in this. This Santa Claus figure, Hope. We need to get him, because what he'll do will be the truly shocking murder.'

# Chapter 17

Clarissa had the hood up on her little green sports car. The windows were closed and the heat was on. Winter wasn't the best for the little car, but it handled the roads well. It was more of a summer thing. A car that you could drive along with the top down, enjoying the sunshine. In winter, the heater fought to keep the car warm inside, and Clarissa was wearing her shawl to reinforce that idea.

She drove to Social Services to see about John Parrish's community service work. She had arrived downtown in Inverness and stood before a large desk and a receptionist that could have been Clarissa's granddaughter.

'Detective Sergeant Clarissa Urquhart,' she said. She had to look at the warrant card for a moment. Of course, she was going to be an inspector, but she wasn't yet. The appointment was soon. Very soon, but not yet.

'What can I do for you?' asked the young girl behind the desk.

'I need to speak to someone about a John Parrish. Someone who does the community service organisation for offenders or previous offenders.'

'Right. If you go down the hall and take a ticket, I'm sure

146

that . . .'

'Take a ticket?' queried Clarissa. 'I'm Detective Sergeant Clarissa Urquhart. I'm here on an investigation, working on a murder case. Get me somebody now.'

'Don't take that tone with me,' said the girl. 'I'm afraid . . .'

'Tone?' said Clarissa. 'Bloody, get me someone.'

'We don't tolerate the abuse of staff here. We don't . . .'

'Abuse to staff?' said Clarissa. 'I haven't even started. Get me someone who can help me. Otherwise, I'll get down here with a squad of people and we'll rip through everything you're doing. The boss can ask why he's getting so much hassle and I'll point him right at you.'

The girl sat down in her seat. 'I'm not taking that sort of language,' she said.

'Fine,' said Clarissa. 'I'll find these people myself.' She turned and barged through a set of double doors. The girl, calling after her, suddenly panicked. Clarissa strode along the corridor, looking at the door signs. She saw one for community service. Marching that way, she burst through another set of double doors into an open plan office.

'Detective Sergeant Clarissa Urquhart; your reception is useless. I need somebody to tell me about community service, particularly for previous offenders, and how it's organised.'

A man stood up. 'If you want to come this way,' he said. 'There's a meeting room in there. Let's talk about what you need.' Behind her, Clarissa heard the receptionist barging in.

'It's fine, Amy, I've got it.'

Clarissa went into the office and sat down with the man sitting opposite. He had a pad and a pencil.

'I'm interested in John Parrish,' said Clarissa, her tone less severe now.

'John Parrish. My name is Eamon, and I'll find out about John Parrish for you.'

'He goes to Drumnadrochit to Marion Burns.'

'One of Marion's ones? Okay, she's quite good with people who are a bit different. It must mean that Mr Parrish is a bit, well, let's say, detached.'

'Really?' said Clarissa.

'Indeed. One second.' The man disappeared outside. He then reappeared five minutes later with a file. As he entered, he looked around the room. 'Is Amy not here again? Has she not . . .'

'Nobody's come in,' said Clarissa.

The man disappeared outside again, but not before he handed Clarissa a file. She opened it and saw a picture of John Parrish. He looked like quite a muscular individual. He had neatly cropped hair, but his face looked gormless. Then again, most people look gormless in photos they are posing for to be stuck in files.

She took a photograph of the photo and one of the files in front of her. John Parrish had been an offender and was in rehabilitation. He'd stolen things. The file said he was low risk, but he was also low intelligence to where he didn't understand the effect he had on other people. Namely, he often found things funny which were completely inappropriate.

Clarissa looked up as the door opened again. Amy walked in and placed a cup of coffee in front of Clarissa.

'That's for you,' the girl said, almost dropping the coffee onto the table.

Clarissa turned and smiled. 'Thank you, my dear. That's very kind of you. I've got everything I want, thank you. Your colleague was most helpful.'

The girl eyed her suspiciously as she left the room, and Clarissa hoped she hadn't spat in the coffee. She took a sip. She didn't know how to be a receptionist, and she didn't know how to make coffee either. Clarissa stopped herself before disparaging the girl any further.

Eamon returned and sat down.

'It says here,' said Clarissa, 'that John Parrish has social issues. He doesn't understand other people.'

'I think that's correct. I met him once. He's not one of the ones that I deal with. I remember somebody scalded themselves with a coffee in the office, and they'd run and put it under the tap. John thought it was hilarious. He's also very strong. I had trouble once with him. He disagreed with moving a piece of furniture, and he grabbed someone, and though he didn't quite break their wrist, it was severely bruised.'

'Marion Burns, who he goes to see? Is she quite strong then?'

'Marion can handle most people, but she's not physically strong. She's clever. She knows how to play the likes of John.'

'Any other particular interests he's got?'

'No. Not to be aware of. He lives up in Social Housing flats. That's the last known address I've got for him,' said Eamon. 'I believe he's still there. He's living off a bit of benefit and his community service. We're hoping we can get him rehabilitated into some sort of warehouse job or something. That would suit his talents. Tire him out through the day, and he's physically strong to take things like that on board. The last thing he needs to be doing is sitting around. He gets ideas, you see.'

'Dangerous ideas?' asked Clarissa.

'Not so far. I mean, as an offender, he was stealing things. He was violent about it. Not overly. Just when the shopkeepers would look to take the items back, he'd refuse. He threw the odd punch, but it would have seemed a lot worse,' said Eamon.

Clarissa thanked the man, left most of the coffee in the cup, and gave Amy a smile as she left the building. The girl better never apply for a job at the police, especially if Clarissa was the one doing the interviews.

She got into her green car and through heavy snow drove to the Social Housing flats that were located towards the centre of the city. They were a grey affair, rather dull, and had three floors. Clarissa entered the building via the front door, let in by one of the other occupants. She then made her way up to the flat of John Parrish and buzzed the door. 'Who's that?'

'DS Clarissa Urquhart. I need to have a word with you, Mr Parrish.'

'I don't know you.'

'No, you don't,' said Clarissa, 'but I've been finding out about you, and we need to talk.'

The intercom went silent. Clarissa stood for what seemed like a minute and got no reply.

'Mr Parrish,' she said. 'Mr Parrish.' Again, there was no response. Clarissa buzzed the flat again.

'Who's this?'

'This is still DS Clarissa Urquhart.'

'Who's DS?'

'Detective Sergeant. It's the police, Mr Parrish. I need to speak to you. I require that you open the door, please.'

'You just said you wanted to speak to me. You can do that with the intercom.

'Mr Parrish, no, please open the door so I don't have to kick it in.'

'Don't kick it in,' he said. The door in front of her suddenly opened, and Clarissa looked up at a six-foot four man. It was a boy's face, but he was an absolute brute. The arms looked like they could crush sofas or rip telephone directories without even looking at them.

'You don't look like a policewoman. You've got no uniform on.'

'I'm a detective sergeant. We don't wear a uniform,' said Clarissa.

'You like those people off the telly, then?'

'Yes,' said Clarissa. She hoped to God she was nothing like anybody off the telly.

'Can we go in and sit down?'

'Okay,' he said. The man stepped to one side, letting Clarissa through. She didn't ask, but walked ahead through a door into a living room. There was a large screen TV with a seat directly in front of it. She saw a games console sitting there. The screen said *Winter Slay Bells*, and she could hear a jingling, like at the start of some sort of Christmas song.

She looked around her. There were snowmen everywhere. A Christmas tree in the corner, but the snowmen dominated. Most people had decorations, and yes, everyone was there. Santa, Rudolph, the elves, Frosty, too. Some had lots of angels. Nativity scene, but this room was snowmen and snowmen only. She couldn't even see any Santa Claus.

'Did you enjoy that game?' said Clarissa.

'It's brilliant, isn't it?' said John. 'I'm the snowman in it. I love being the snowman. Have you ever been the snowman in it?'

'The snowman's not what I do,' said Clarissa. 'What's it like playing the snowman?'

'I nearly won,' said John. 'I nearly won. It was a long game, and I forgot . . . I forgot to ring the bells. I forgot to ring the bells before I did it.'

There was a ringing of bells, Clarissa thought, before the attack by the Krampus. There were no bells in either of the others. He just said that he'd forgotten, and if John was the snowman, that tallied up. The CCTV didn't show the snowman ringing any bells. The elf may have done. Maybe Maddie had done, but there was nobody there, except for the one person who couldn't report it afterwards, Alice Greenwood. She'd been slaughtered.

'How did you nearly win?' asked Clarissa.

'Killed him in his shop. Froze him. Froze the man in his shop, but it wasn't his shop, but it was a shop. Froze him to death.'

'But you forgot the bells.'

The man almost looked glum. 'Not just that. I got them to film it, but they didn't show it. They never showed it on the TV.'

'Did you do anything else?'

'Oh, I've been the elf. I've been the elf and I shot someone. I've been Santa, too.'

'Where did you work as Santa and the elf?'

'Jinglesville,' he said. 'But they let me come to Inverness for the snowman one. It's easier when you understand the place. You know where you are; you know where you can get things,' said John Parrish.'

*He's actually admitting to this. He doesn't realise, but he's admitting to this*, thought Clarissa. *I'm going to have to play this coyly. We need to bring him in, but he's a heck of a size of a guy.*

'How did you dress up as the snowman?' asked Clarissa.

'Through here,' said the man. He took Clarissa through to his

152

bedroom and there, sitting on the floor, was a large snowman's outfit.

'I kept it elsewhere,' he said, 'because you have to for the game. Nobody's allowed to see it. Nobody knows it's you and him. But my game's over now, so it doesn't matter—you can see it.'

Clarissa went over but didn't touch it. 'I see you've got a smiley mouth on the head, but there's no nose. How did you—'

'The nose is through here. Mrs, Burns, she says that this nose, it's good to eat, delicious.'

'Are you chopping it up?' said Clarissa.

'Yes,' he said. 'There was a bit on the end that was broken, but I put that in the bin. He turned and walked back to the living room and played the game. Clarissa stood in his kitchen and took out an evidence bag from her pocket. She sifted through the bin until she found the broken end of a carrot. A clean chop on one side, broken on the other. She labelled up the bag and then took out her mobile phone.'

'Hope,' she said, 'you will not believe this, but I've found number two. Our snowman is here. He's not exactly confessed, but he's told me all about it. We're going to need to get Social Services with us. He's not the full shilling. I'm not even sure he's realised he's killed a real person, or even what that means.'

After arranging for units to come down and for Social Services to meet them, Clarissa stood at the entrance to the kitchen. She looked at the snowman-covered living room, and at the might of John Parrish playing *Winter Slay Bells*. Clarissa didn't usually feel anything for those who had committed murders. If anything, it was repulsion. Looking at this man now, she only felt sympathy. Somebody had led this poor child up the garden path. She was going to find out who, and she was going to make them pay.

# Chapter 18

Macleod was tired and the snow outside seemed to bring an icy chill to his bones despite sitting in the warm office. The press conference had been rough. It was the usual cavalcade. *Were the police doing enough?* And without taking them through every bit of the case, Macleod couldn't prove that they were. They were on top of everything, but such details couldn't be shared.

Ross was knee-deep in searching the computers and other electronic devices of Maddie Jefferson. Clarissa was bringing in John Parrish and trying to elicit from him as much detail as possible, although Macleod was unsure how much that would be. Cunningham was searching Maddie Jefferson's house. Again, another sensible idea, but just what was going to happen from it, he didn't know.

And yet, he wondered just exactly how much he trusted Cunningham. Completely was the answer, of course. This grey figure was just messing with his head when he spoke such evil statements in his mind, but he'd go. Macleod was convinced he would go.

He heard the thump on the stairs, and then his door was flung open. There was no knock as Hope McGrath bounded into the office, her red ponytail flapping crazily behind her.

'Seoras, they've got Lyle. Lyle's been grabbed.'

'They are? Just one of them?'

'Solo attacker. I need to get a manhunt going. Start doing a search out from . . .'

'Yes,' said Macleod, 'Go, go. Go organise. It's not a problem. Just get on with it. I'll cover off any media or anything else.'

Hope nodded and turned on her heel, bounding back out of the door, but leaving it open. After a moment, his secretary came across and went to close the door.

'Just a moment,' said Macleod. 'Get Constable Williams for me, can you? I need to talk to him.'

'Of course, Seoras,' said his secretary and disappeared down the stairs. A few minutes later, Constable Williams entered the office and Macleod indicated he should close the door behind him.

'We've just had Mr Lyle taken. He was the one who was unsuccessfully whipped the other night. Well, he was successfully whipped. They just didn't kill him. The Krampus had grabbed him. Apparently, he's been grabbed again. I think this is to finish him off,' said Macleod.

He saw the constable swallow. 'I know that's quite unpalatable, but with your understanding of the game, I want to know, are there specific options for the Krampus disposing of people?'

'Wow,' said Williams, 'There's quite a lot.'

'Run me through them,' said Macleod.

'Well, I mean, one of the obvious ones is whipping them. I think that comes from the history of the Krampus, that it comes with Birch, but you can also spear them, that's one. You can run them over in a car.'

'A car? Won't it just crash into them?' asked Macleod.

'No, you actually have to run them over in a certain way and in a certain place so that most people get to see it.'

'Are there any other sort of more gruesome ideas?'

'There's quite a few. I mean, you can shoot them,' said Williams.

'What gets you the most points, though? What's the biggest way to kill somebody in the game?'

'Well,' said Williams, 'It's bizarre. You have to run the person over with a sleigh and you decapitate them.' Williams looked almost embarrassed.

'You play this?'

'I do, but you also have to do it,' said Williams, 'somewhere very public.'

'Thank you,' said Macleod, and watched as Williams departed. Macleod stood up, exited the office, and walked down the stairs. Beside him walked a man in a grey monk's habit. He was whispering to Macleod that he didn't have a hope in hell of finding out where Lyle had gone. He was telling him that Lyle was as good as dead, mentioning all the different ways to kill him. Macleod was ignoring him and made his way down to the cafeteria.

Once there, he ordered a coffee and took a seat. After ten minutes, he'd finished the coffee, and he walked back upstairs. He looked out of his office window, not his favourite view these days, and the man in the grey habit stood beside him.

'You don't know, Macleod. You've no idea. Another one's going to die because of you. You haven't got a clue.'

Macleod turned and looked into the hood of the man beside him. There should have been a face in there to see, but there was nothing.

'Decapitation with a sleigh,' said Macleod. The shopping centre. He remembered the shopping centre. There was a sleigh there. It was in the middle of what would be a packed area. There was a sleigh up a small slope. *How could it be used?*

Macleod spat the word shopping centre into the face, leaning into the hood of the figure in the grey habit. Quickly he walked from behind his desk, threw on his coat, went out, announcing to the secretary that he was off on a hunch.

He marched down into the office looking for Hope, but of course, she was off organising a manhunt. There were some constables still working away, but Ross had gone as well. Patterson was there, and Macleod strode over to him.

'You need to come with me. We're off to the shopping centre.'

'Why?' asked Patterson.

Of course, he hadn't been out of the office. Not since the incident. Not since his throat had been cut. He was desk-bound. He was meant to be desk-bound.

'I think someone's going to die,' said Macleod. 'I need you now.'

Patterson stood up, went for his coat, and followed Macleod down to the car. Macleod drove, and he could see that Patterson was agitated sitting beside him. On arrival at the shopping centre, Macleod parked the car in the centre car park, ran out, and took the grey concrete steps up to the floor with the shops.

'Whereabouts are we going?' asked Patterson, following.

'There was a display. There's a display in the shopping centre,' said Macleod.

'You'll never find it,' said a man in a grey monk's habit who'd appeared at the corner. The shoppers seemed to ignore the figure, but some were recognising Macleod.

'There's a sleigh, Patterson. It's in the shopping centre. I haven't been in here in three weeks, but they put it up.'

'Okay,' said Patterson, 'I think it's down the other end.'

'Then let's go. Come on.'

Macleod didn't exactly run, but he was walking briskly, occasionally breaking out into a trot. Patterson was struggling to keep up. He saw the display, the sleigh at the top, and it had a slope that the sleigh came down. The sleigh currently was above head height, but the bottom of the display reached down to where people could stand. It was meant to be Santa bringing presents down, and there were little snowmen arranged at the bottom. Macleod thought it looked a little on the ridiculous side, but he thought a lot about Christmas was ridiculous.

On the other side of the display was a jewellery store and a camping shop. 'He'll be about here,' said Macleod. 'If I'm right, he'll be about here.'

Macleod glanced up and sitting on the sleigh was the guy in the monk's habit. 'You're in the wrong place. He's going to die.'

Macleod fought himself, managing not to shout at the man in the grey monk's habit. Instead, turning to Paterson, he said, 'We need to look for the Krampus.'

'Isn't he going to stick out?' asked Paterson. 'How does he get here?'

'Exactly. How do you get here? Where do you come from? Are there back ways in these shops? You go into the jewellery store. I'm going to go to this camping shop. From there we can work down, gradually work out away from the shops that are beside the display.'

'Okay, and I'm looking for a Krampus?'

'Or a way to get in. Can you come in through the back of

159

the shop? There might be. Ask. Go on,' said Macleod.

He tore off into the camping shop, looking around for an assistant. There was a man standing behind the counter, and Macleod walked over to him, whipping out his warrant card. 'I'm Detective Chief Inspector Macleod,' he said. 'Is there another way into the shop other than that front entrance? Can you come in through the back?'

'Well, you can do,' he said.

'You need to show me. You need to show me now.'

'Hey, you're the guy from the TV. You've been doing the TV announcements, haven't you? Is this about the killings? Is this about . . .'

'Shut up,' said Macleod, 'and show me the back of your shop now. I'm in a hurry. Show me!'

The man's face went almost white, and immediately he turned and raced off towards the back of the shop. He opened the door there, and Macleod walked in. There was a small store area, and then a back passage.

'Where does this go?' he asked.

'We can get down to the car park. We can do deliveries through the back,' said the man.

'Lock this door.'

'Lock it?' queried the man. 'But that's also like a fire escape. I can't—'

'I am telling you to lock it. And I'll come back and tell you when to unlock it. Right now, I'm saying lock this door.'

Macleod's face looked like thunder, and the man obeyed. Macleod turned and strode back out of the camping shop. He looked over at the jewellery store. There was a figure there with curled horns. It had hair coming down from its jowls. It was the figure that he'd seen on the television. The figure that

160

had invaded the stage. It was the Krampus, and it was dragging Ernest Lyle with it. The man looked woozy, almost drugged, and it wasn't much of an effort for the Krampus to pull him across. Macleod went to run out of the camping shop, but just as he did, a group of ladies walked in. He clattered into them.

'What are you doing? Get out of the way,' said one woman, hitting him with an umbrella.

'Police, get out of the way,' said Macleod, fighting to push through.

'You don't look like the police.'

'Yes, he does,' said another woman. 'That's him off the telly!'

Macleod shoved her as gently as he could, but with enough force to push her to one side. The Krampus was reaching the display, and Macleod saw Patterson running after it. He was big, and Macleod thought Patterson was going to struggle. He thought about going to help him, thought about joining in.

Patterson looked white, but to give the man his due, he ran at the Krampus. There was a punch from the Krampus that hit Patterson in the face. He stumbled for a moment, then threw himself, driving his shoulder at the Krampus's body. The Krampus reached down and pushed him off with one hand. He still had Lyle in the other, and dragged him across, pushing him to the front of the display.

The display had tracks running down from the sleigh to the front of it. In the display, those tracks were deep grooves, and Macleod could see that the sleigh would run down them to the front. *Was it designed to do that?* He hadn't had time to examine it properly.

The Krampus took Lyle, pushed him down, and Macleod saw that the track of the sleigh would go right across the neck of Lyle. Lyle was so woozy, he didn't even seem to fight.

161

Patterson jumped again at the Krampus, and for a moment was tugging at the face. He'd pulled it down by the horn, yanking at it, and Macleod thought about helping him, but he disappeared round the back of the display. Patterson felt a blow to the stomach and hung on to the horn. Another one forced him to release, and he was pushed back by the Krampus, which then drove a boot into his stomach. It knocked the wind out of Patterson, and he tried to call out for security. Around him, he could hear yells and screams.

'Stop him,' yelled Patterson. 'You've got to stop him.'

The Krampus was now reaching over towards the complicated set of wires that held the sleigh in place. He was pulling at one, untying it. Patterson got up, out of breath, staggered forward to the Krampus, but was knocked back down with a kick.

'Would somebody get him? Stop him from doing it.'

Patterson saw the surrounding terror, people in panic. The Krampus was pulling at the string, the wires that held the sleigh. One snapped, then a second. There was only one up above, but the Krampus had it within reach. He reached over, pulled at it, undoing it from the hook that held it to the sleigh.

Patterson stood in shock as the sleigh descended. There were screams from all around. The sleigh's blade was running down the gutter. It was going to go across the neck of an incredibly docile Ernest Lyle.

Patterson turned his head away, not wanting to see the man's decapitation, but then there was a cry of shock from the crowd. Patterson looked back quickly. It wasn't a shock at an abhorrent sight. It was the fact that the sleigh had stopped.

The Krampus reached for it, trying to pull. Security was arriving, and Macleod appeared from behind the sleigh, yelling at them to take the Krampus down. With the aid of about five men, the Krampus was put to the ground, and Patterson secured handcuffs on it. Macleod was over at Ernest Lyle, Patterson walking towards him, looking bemused.

'Well done, Constable,' said Macleod. 'You kept him engaged. You've saved this man's life.'

'Aye, but it's . . . look at it. How's it still hanging up there? He took off all the wires. He—'

Macleod led Patterson round the back of it. Attached to the sleigh was a hose. It had been wrapped around the sleigh's frame, and Patterson looked to where that hose was wrapped around a pillar.

'It slid down more than I thought it would,' said Macleod, 'but it did it. I would never be strong enough to tackle him, but you kept him from carrying out the deed long enough that we did it. Well done, Patterson. After all you've been through, that was so well done.'

# Chapter 19

Ross set up an entire table of printed notes scanned from the originals from Maddie's house. Cunningham had searched long and hard, along with her team of uniformed officers. Beneath the floorboards, they had found various notes which now adorned Ross's table. Mixed in with these were the computer records that the geeks downstairs had rescued from Maddie's devices. They had begun looking through them on the twenty-third of December, and it had now rolled into Christmas Eve morning.

Ross was exhausted, but he could feel the tension coming from the boss's office. Both Hope and Macleod were getting it in the neck from higher up, and the team was creaking under the stress. There was a consensus that any attacks would be carried out either before or on Christmas Day. Now there were fewer than forty-eight hours left.

'This is the one I don't get,' said Cunningham. 'She's made a note.'

'Have you taken it down and asked her about it?'

'Maddie Jefferson is saying nothing. She won't say anything until Boxing Day. Until the deed is done and then she'll tell us the lot. You'd better believe it,' said Cunningham. She was standing behind a desk, hands on her hips, ponytail tied up behind her. She shook her head and altered the ponytail, making it somewhat tighter. Ross laughed.

'What?' she asked.

'That's what Hope does. Whenever she's stressed out, she messes about with her ponytail.'

'I'm not just a Hope clone. You realise that, don't you?'

'Very much,' said Ross. 'It's very easy when you're down at the bottom here to be forgotten about. Everybody always talked about Macleod. Macleod's cleverness. When Kirsten joined us, she was as clever, if not more so. She could think in ways he didn't. In fairness to him, he loved that about her.'

'And she's the one that went off to be a secret agent?'

'Operative,' said Ross. 'Operative is the word. She'd been working in Lewis when we first met her, but she came back over here. Her brother passed on, but he was in some sort of a care home or something, an institute. He wasn't quite able to live life on his own.'

'But you said I'm not like Hope.'

'You are in some mannerisms. When Hope first started, Macleod thought she was quite a loose woman.'

Cunningham raised her eyebrows.

'Well, you've got the rumours about you that go round the station. I have seen no evidence of it, though.'

'I'm not easy, if that's what you're saying.'

'It's not what I'm saying,' said Ross, 'and trust me, I've no particular interest in whether or not you are, but you're certainly very dedicated and you think well. I reckon you think differently from Hope. You're not just a by-the-book girl.'

Cunningham smiled. 'No,' she said, 'but this bit here, this bit here where they talk about a great, a grandiose thing, that's coming from Santa Claus. He's the one that's going to go out with a bang. He's going to be the one who shows them all.

'So far we've got Maddie Jefferson,' continued Susan. 'She seems quite impressionable. John Parish is a bit of a sorry case in some ways. Been let down, been manipulated. Our Krampus is now locked up and is saying absolutely nothing. We don't even know who he is at the moment.

'You've got to be a bit of a nutjob though, haven't you?' mused Cunningham. 'He wanted to decapitate someone in a shopping centre, in front of kids and everybody. I mean, it's bizarre. It's like something you'd hear . . .'

'What? Overseas? Middle East, Asian, something like that?' said Ross.

'What did he have against Lyle?'

Ross continued to type away on his keyboard, and Cunningham wondered what he was looking at this time.

'What are you doing?'

'Well, we have two IP addresses that were being searched several times from some of Maddie's devices. If they were all working with each other and covering off details about their proposed attacks, she may have been researching for the other ones. There may be some details about places they wanted to look at.'

'What's the address it's showing, though?'

'Come round here,' said Ross. Susan Cunningham stepped round, put her hand on Ross's shoulder, looking over it at the screen in front of the two of them. 'It's the superstore, this one,' he said.

'I can see that, but what are they going to do in there? It's very general, isn't it? Just a superstore. There's a ton of information on there. I guess we can phone in and see if they've got any problems with the staff. Look at it that way.'

'The other one I think's is a butcher's,' said Ross. He tapped on the keyboard again and up it came.

'Definitely a butcher's,' said Cunningham. 'That looks like it could be quite a small team, though. I mean, not that many targets. It might be easier to go after that one. I'll get on the phone and see what's going on with them.'

The day was getting close to midday, and Susan Cunningham hoped she'd still get a response. The thing about butchers close to Christmas was they would not sell that much after lunch. Most of them did big orders for people who ordered their meat in advance. Very few people were shopping last minute for their turkey or meat on Christmas Eve. It might be last-minute things like the milk, or they'd forgotten the sprouts. Usually, it was a daft thing, not the stuff for the Christmas meal.

'Hello,' said a voice on the other end of the phone. 'You've got through to Jonno's Butcher's. How can we help?'

'This is DC Cunningham. I was hoping to come down and meet your staff to have a word with them.'

'Our staff? Is there something up?'

'Well, we'd just like to talk. Your business has been flagged regarding a murder investigation. We're not suggesting that you've done anything awry, but we are worried that you could be some sort of target.'

'Seriously? Well, nobody's going to be coming into the shop. I'm just about to lock up. We go out for a staff party on Christmas Eve because they work so hard up to it. Everybody from the staff will be there, but that's not kicking off until tonight. We give them this afternoon off to run any errands they've got, sort themselves out before the big day tomorrow.'

'Your party tonight, can you give me the address of it?'

'Okay, but we take a minibus.'

'Where do you start out?' asked Cunningham.

'Well, we collect everyone from the shop here in the minibus. We'll all be there. I don't think it's anything to do with our business. We all get on really well. I don't understand why you're looking at us. I have had no employee trouble in years. They get time off around Christmas. We give them the big Christmas treat at the end.'

'I'm not saying there is something definitely up,' said Cunningham. 'It's just you've been flagged through our investigation, and I need to take precautions. We'll pop down to see you when you're heading off.'

'We'll be there tonight, five o'clock outside our shop.' Susan Cunningham made her way back to the table. Standing in front of it, she reached up and adjusted her ponytail. Then she saw Ross looking at her.

'No, it didn't go that well. Doesn't seem to be a company that has any issues, but it's all we've got, so I better check it out.'

'We've got the superstore as well. I'm going to look through staff records on both companies. Hope and the big boss will want to know what we're doing and what's going on. Can you cover that?' asked Ross.

Susan Cunningham exited the office, seeing that Hope's smaller office was empty. Climbing the stairs to Macleod's, she wondered if that's where everyone was. As she approached the secretary, Cunningham was advised that Macleod was interviewing Maddie Jefferson with Hope again. Clarissa had been looking for him as well.

Cunningham made her way down to the canteen and saw Clarissa sitting with Patterson. The man had a coffee before him, but his hands were trembling.

'Are you two okay?' asked Cunningham, walking over.

'You getting anywhere?' asked Clarissa.

'No. I was just going to see the big boss to tell him about some plans. Ross has got a couple of contacts we need to check out, but we'll do that this evening. I'm not sure that we're able to do anything positive.'

'Well, I doubt you'll see Macleod or Hope for a while. They're going to have a crack at that Krampus character. He's still not saying who he is or anything about himself,' said Clarissa.

'Are you all right, Patterson?' asked Susan. 'You look . . . well, you look a bit . . .'

'Peaky. He's just a bit peaky,' said Clarissa. 'Let's go up and get something to eat,' she said to Cunningham. She took the woman by the arm, herding her over towards the canteen area.

'I'm not even hungry,' said Cunningham.

'Just buy something,' said Clarissa. 'Otherwise, he'll know it's a ruse.'

'Is he okay?'

'No. Macleod took him out from behind the safety of his desk because there was no one else there. He then walks into the Krampus and the sleigh, coming down to cut off Ernest Lyle's head. Got kicked to the ground several times. He's just a bit traumatised by it. He could do with getting out of the murder squad. Patterson's like me; he's not made for it.'

'You're made for it,' said Cunningham. 'You're dogged, you're determined.'

'But I can't put the murders out of my head. You have to be able to go home at night and sleep. When I was doing the art cases, I saw some nasty stuff, don't get me wrong, because people in that world can intimidate with the best of them.

There was even the odd killing, but not like it is here. Not when it's your day job. The time I saw the kids . . .' Clarissa shook her head. 'There's a reason I'm moving on. I also nearly saw the boss killed. I've taken a battering.'

'Why don't you just retire?' asked Cunningham.

'Because it's in my bones. It's in your bones too, I can tell,' said Clarissa. 'You take a bit of advice from me. Don't become somebody's image. Don't become somebody who's just a replica of another figure. Hope's fabulous, she's a good boss, but she doesn't know when to go off on a tangent. When to just say 'stuff this' and get it done.

'I had to save Macleod's arse. Had to break it all open. I had to get out of the standard loop. Don't become a Hope clone because she wouldn't have done that. He'd have been dead. Be your own woman. You're lucky,' said Clarissa; 'you've got looks. You've got a friendly disposition. Seem to get on well with people. I have a temper, a bloody-mindedness, but I use it. Use it to get what needs done, and rub people up the wrong way.'

'You seem to be helping him, though,' said Susan, nodding at Patterson.

'Patterson's quite a refined figure. I don't know what he's doing in the murder squad. He's clever and yet he's sitting behind a desk working on reports, cross-referencing. Ross is better at that than he is. Patterson should be out digging. He can dig, he really can, just needs to learn a bit. Get the green off him.

'Patterson can connect with people when he wants to. He's come from quite a posh background and has a polite way of talking to people. But he gets what needs to be done. I saw that, though he wound me up. In the short time he was with me, he might have questioned things, but when he saw it and he saw it for what it was, he followed me.

'I didn't hang on to that throat of his, didn't stop that blood pumping just so he could be some office jerk kicking about, getting told to look up this, look up that. That's a detective right there, and if he stays here, Macleod isn't going to use him that way because Macleod's too detached from him, not working with him enough. Hope's going to be by the book, holding him back medically. Especially after this episode with Macleod. He needs a fresh start.'

'You might be right,' said Cunningham, 'but what I need is to find the bosses and update them. We need to get out tonight, not be sitting in here. I've got two leads even if they're very loose. Hopefully by dinner time, or even before, Ross might have narrowed us down with some better line to go on. But if he hasn't, it's time to push things about, as they say.'

'Well, you go push him,' said Clarissa. 'You go push him. I'll tell Patterson you weren't hungry.'

'No,' said Cunningham. 'I am now. Tell him I'm taking it up to Ross. That man needs to know when to eat as well.'

# Chapter 20

Susan Cunningham sat in the car, tapping her foot beside the accelerator pedal. She had told Hope that she was going down to the car, ready to head out to the butcher's shop that she had discovered earlier with Ross. They'd be going on their night out. They were departing at five.

Cunningham was looking at a clock that said ten to the hour. Surely, they might be a few minutes late in getting away because people did that, but it was heavy snow tonight and the roads wouldn't be great. Cunningham sat and tapped the wheel of the car with her fingers, drumming them. She wished she was going out tonight, socially, not hunting killers.

She'd had an offer. One constable had said if she wasn't doing anything, he wouldn't mind taking her out to one of the clubs. She was busy working, though. One thing Susan had discovered was she wasn't missing it. It was unfair what they said about her. That she was promiscuous was the polite word. Taken out by everyone. The Force bike, some of them put it, which was downright rude and wrong. But she had been someone who enjoyed one-night stands, and she'd had quite a few of them. Now that she was working, she discovered she didn't miss them. It was almost as if her dates were simply something to do.

She looked back over the last couple of years and realised she hadn't had a proper relationship. Part of her didn't regret that. She wasn't looking for one. She just wondered why she filled life up with meaningless ones in between. Almost as if she needed the physicality. Maybe she could find the physicality elsewhere. Take up a sport.

Susan looked out of the car window. She hadn't been on holiday. Not a proper holiday for a long while. The last one was three years ago. She'd been paid to go on holiday with a guy she'd met in the club. It had been fine. She'd had a lot of fun, but it was a holiday where she had seen nothing except the terrace of the villa they were staying in and the bedroom.

She was more than that. He hadn't found that out. She hadn't forced the issue so he would either. She would wake up tomorrow morning in her own house. There wasn't even a Christmas tree up. She hadn't wanted to decorate until it was a lot later. When the case kicked off, she ended up working and not doing it at all. It was all right, though. She'd probably be back in here tomorrow.

The car door opened, and she saw Hope's long legs, clad in her dark black jeans, slip into the footwell of the passenger seat.

'Let's go,' said Hope. Susan started up the car.

'Cutting it fine,' said Susan.

'I had to brief everyone. It's difficult keeping on top. We need to keep the communications going tonight as well because we are stretched if they all try to kill at once.'

Of course, Susan understood that. She was just frustrated by an awful lot of things. It took ten minutes to drive to the butcher's, and the time was two minutes past five when they arrived.

Outside the front of the shop was a minibus, which looked three-quarters full. As they pulled up in the car, the snow was still falling. Susan wrapped her jacket around her. In truth, she was probably underdressed. She had packed warmer clothes in the boot as they would be inside following this crowd. As she arrived at the minibus, Susan realised she was probably overdressed by comparison.

'Hello,' said a fat, jolly man, 'I'm Daniel, the boss of the place. How are you doing? You must have been the one who rang earlier on.'

Susan pulled out her warrant card. 'I'm DC Susan Cunningham. This is my boss, Detective Inspector—'

'Hope McGrath,' said the man, smiling. 'Sorry,' he said. 'I've had a couple already. Got the minibus, you see. Don't have to worry about the drink. You're that one off the telly,' he said. 'Better looking than that bloke. Sorry, shouldn't have said that. Bit forward.' He turned and looked around him.

'How much have you had?' Susan asked.

'Oh, well, there's a bottle of wine that's now empty. We started quite early. Don't worry, I'll still be going by the end of the evening. It's been a crazy Christmas. Busiest we've ever had. I've worked right through, but the staff, they've had time off.'

'Has everyone been happy about that?'

'Delighted. They're all getting a big bonus. They're all getting a night out on me. All the drinks are free. Look, here's Jemma.'

Susan turned to see Jemma standing beside her.

'Blimey, Jemma. You could have brought a coat.'

'We're going to be inside. I'm not cold.'

Susan looked at the woman who could only be in her very

early twenties. Susan wasn't prudish. She could wear clothes that were skimpy or provocative. But she wore them in the right place. Certainly, she wouldn't have come out tonight without a coat on, even if she was thinking a club outfit was okay for later on.

Daniel was definitely slightly tipsy. His stare at the girl lingered just a little too long before he turned back to Susan.

'As I said, everybody's happy. You can ask Donna there.'

He pointed over at a woman who was maybe towards her early thirties. She was of average height for a woman, but she had curves and she knew how to use them. There was a jolly look on her face that showed her resemblance to her father. As she approached, Susan could see that a few of the male employees were giving her the eye and she wasn't averse to giving it back, especially the younger lads. Two of them were walking along the street, approaching her. Donna put her arms out, allowing them to link up with her.

'Are you sure you're going to handle the both of us?' said the young lad.

'I'll handle you both and have you back to your mums before bedtime,' said Donna, 'because that's about all you'll last with me.'

Daniel laughed, roaring loudly, and the two boys smiled. Behind, there was another woman who was strolling along with other male employees. She was thinner, taller, and had a more sober look on her face.

'That's Emma, my other daughter,' said Daniel. 'She doesn't go in for the alcohol as much. Said she's got a bit of a rough head tonight. She'll be all right, though. She'll come out with us.'

Several of the men that were walking with her tried approaching Donna, offering to take her arm away from the other boys. Donna seemed to almost tease them, turning them away. Susan thought she could see more than just disappointment in some lads; there was outright annoyance.

Hope cornered Emma off to one side, and Susan joined her.

'You seem to be the sober one here. Can I ask you, have there been any issues with your employees this Christmas? Anybody annoyed? Your father says, everybody seems thrilled with what they're getting, but he is . . . how shall we put it? Slightly inebriated.'

'My father's had plenty to drink, and he deserves it,' said Emma, 'and so do these employees. They've worked very hard, but they've had time off and are getting a bonus. They're getting paid very well. It's been busy. It's been really busy.'

'Some of them look annoyed tonight, though,' said Hope.

'Some of the younger boys. That's Donna for you,' said Emma. 'Several of them are besotted with her. Not just playing at it. It's one thing to flirt. I've done it myself on occasion, but Donna hands out promises. Not to do with the business, just the other sort of promises.'

Emma glowered at Donna. 'A lot of them see her as a good catch. She drives an expensive car into work, wears provocative clothes. She flashes her eyes, makes little quips to them. Boys of that age, they are boys. They're not men yet. Some of them are late teens, some of them early twenties. They're all . . . well, you know how they are. Testosterone flying here, there, and everywhere. Don't get me wrong, they're grand lads. They work hard. We get our money's worth out of them. Some of them are good fun, but you don't offer them that sort of thing. It gets them too excited. It gets them too worked up. Not their fault. Time of life they're in.'

'You clearly don't approve,' said Susan.

'It's going to come to a head,' said Emma. 'There'll be tears, mark my words. People are going to find they've been let down. They're going to find that some people don't take to her parading herself like that or teasing, tempting them.'

Emma's father came over and gave her a large cuddle. 'This one's too serious tonight. She needs to relax. I hope you see there's nothing happening here, officers. You're welcome to come and join us. It's a pity you must work at this time of the year. I feel for you. You do a grand job. Pass on my best wishes to your boss, Seoras. That's it . . . isn't he Seoras Macleod?'

'Seoras,' said Hope. 'Seoras Macleod. I will do, sir. We may follow you, though. So, where's your bus going to?'

He gave the name of a club which Susan recognised and Hope and she waved goodbye. They watched in at the windows of the bus, saw Donna slapping the hands of a few of the guys. There were a few cheeky grabs towards her, and she even planted a kiss on a few of the boys. Emma's face looked like thunder, but the father seemed to just roar with laughter.

'What do you make of it?' asked Susan.

'Nothing looks wrong. Definitely, she's winding those young lads up, but it looks nothing more than office party stuff.'

'I think we should follow,' said Susan. 'We said that it wasn't necessarily just about employees. We have got no other leads, have we? Nobody else to tell. It's not like we can just drive around all evening hoping we come across what's going to happen.'

'No, but I've got the boss looking into the superstore. We could join in there.'

'I don't think so,' said Susan.

'Oh, you don't? You realise I'm the boss?'

'I'm not saying that,' said Susan. 'My judgment would be we need to be here. I think we're in the right place.'

'We're looking for men now. The only discontent is coming from Donna and Emma.'

'We're looking for people of a certain size. Besides, one of the boys could be the killer. A couple of them fit the sizes. They're big enough.'

'Okay,' said Hope. 'We'll start off that way. If we're not seeing anything after watching them for a while down at the club, we'll move on.'

'I am pretty sure,' said Susan.

'Macleod once told me I had to trust the team. I honestly don't agree with you on this one, Susan, but Macleod said before that he didn't always get it right. So, I'm going to give you a chance to see your theory through, but let's go get in the car. I think the one thing we can both agree on is, it's Baltic. How some of them girls can wear those outfits?'

Susan turned away and smiled. Walking back to the car, she felt alive. Hope was going with her idea. It was a time for Susan to make a mark. A time for Susan to show that she could see through people. She could put two and two together about people, assess them the way Macleod could. Oh, she wasn't on that level, not yet, but she was pretty sure about this one.

She opened the car door, stepped inside, turned on the engine, and turned up the fan heater. The hot air blew around her and she pulled out and followed the minibus driving away to the club.

'Have you got anything on tomorrow?' asked Hope.

'I thought I'd probably be in here working.'

'But if you weren't, do you have anything?'

'No, the last three Christmases I've spent at a different man's house. Enjoyed it, don't get me wrong,' said Susan. 'I've been too busy. I was thinking earlier on, I haven't been out with anyone.'

'Is there anyone you fancy? Anyone you actually like?' asked Hope.

'Is this a concern?'

'It's just idle chat,' said Hope. 'You don't have to answer if you don't want to.'

'There's nobody I want,' said Susan. 'I used to just take up with them for a bit of fun. It's nice to wake up on Christmas day and have some guy try to pamper you to get what he wants. I don't feel I want that anymore.'

'Why? Is there someone special?'

'There's no one. I'm quite happy,' she said. 'Quite happy doing what I do.'

'Well, if we crack this, you're welcome over at mine if you don't want to be on your own.'

'Thank you,' said Susan. 'Is there anyone else, or is it just you and John?'

'It's just me and John. That's the plan.'

'Well, in that case, maybe I'll stay on my own, but thanks.'

'No offence taken,' said Hope.

'With all due respect, you want me to sit all day watching some guy have his arms around you while I have no one? I said I didn't miss it. It doesn't mean I won't get jealous looking at it.'

'Well, let's hope you see some badly drunk and divorced behaviour tonight. Then you'll be desperately glad to be on your own tomorrow,' said Hope. She grinned at Susan and the woman laughed back.

# Chapter 21

Macleod and Ross arrived at the superstore a bit before four o'clock, while Hope and Susan Cunningham were tending to the butcher's shop. Using the sizes of the two remaining outfits, Macleod asked the store manager if all the staff who fitted said costumes could be brought to him. He could check whether they were potential suspects from their measurements. One outfit was a size 48 chest and a 40-inch waist with long legs. Macleod knew they would be looking for a rather large person for that. The other outfit was much smaller. If there ever was going to be a Santa, he was going to be a big lad.

The manager of the store was unhappy, complaining it was Christmas Eve and they were open till five. Right now, this was a great inconvenience. At the last minute, when everything needed to be put away so everyone could get out for their Christmas Eve parties, Macleod was insisting on wasting his time.

'I don't feel it's a waste of time, sir,' said Macleod. 'We're investigating a murder, in fact, several, and all to do with the trade around Inverness. Forgive me if you can't get out for your festive glass of eggnog. I'll be working on this a lot longer than you will.'

Ross wasn't sure that this eased the tensions between Macleod and the store manager. Maybe if they came up with a potential lead, the justification would be there for all to see. Members of the staff breezed in and sat before Macleod and Ross. On each step through the door, Ross would pull a sheet of paper with details about them he'd found out from store records and from other personal records. He'd been working fast that day. Not all profiles were complete, but at least it was a starting point. Macleod questioned each member of the staff. They seemed like ordinary, everyday people.

There seemed to be no one of genuine interest. All seemed happy enough in their job. Maybe that was because it was Christmas Eve, and they were about to be off for a day or two, or maybe it was because they were covering something up. Macleod couldn't see a killer amongst them. Ross hadn't seen it either in the profiles he'd drawn up. As he combed through the list of workers, they came to the end of those present at the store. Ross placed another three pieces of paper on the table and Macleod looked at them.

There were two women, one nearly in her sixties, another one, early twenties. They may have fitted the Badalisc outfit, but they certainly wouldn't have fitted Santa Claus. Unlike the man in the third piece of paper. His name was Thomas Wilson. According to Ross's details, he wasn't local to the area. He'd been working up here for a year and a half. When Macleod brought the manager in to talk about him, the man seemed rather agitated.

'Big Tommy. Big Tommy quit not that long ago. Awkward man. Very awkward man to work with. Every time you wanted to ask for a bit of overtime from him, he couldn't do it for this reason, couldn't do it for that reason. He wanted you to sort out all his time off. He always won. Had kids, I believe, down in Newcastle. You can't just pop down to Newcastle every two minutes, can you? I think it took him about a day to get there, a day to get back, and then he'd want to have two, three, four days with them.'

Ross could see why Tommy would have a problem with this manager.

'"That's all right," I said. "Go and use your annual leave." He expected that every time he put a request in for it, he would get it. Then he wanted more days beyond it. He would go sick, and you wouldn't see him for five or six days. Always found out where he was. He was down in Newcastle. He seemed to think that was his right.'

'What was he like as a worker when he was here, though, doing the actual job?' asked Macleod.

'He worked in the warehouse at the back, bringing all the stuff through. He's a massive guy. Massive.'

'You say he quit in the end. What was the final straw? What do you think made him finally take the step? It sounds like for a long while you were having issues with him, and he wasn't getting what he wanted.'

'I couldn't give him Christmas off,' said the manager. 'I couldn't give him Christmas. He said that was a problem because he couldn't then get down to Newcastle. He'd miss Christmas Day with the kids. I remember it because he threw an absolute wobbly.'

'In what way?' asked Macleod.

'Came into the office, and picked up a file, threw it off the wall. He was ready to hit me. I swear he was ready to hit me, but he didn't. It was almost like he just stopped.'

'When was this?'

'Probably about a month ago.'

Macleod turned and looked at Ross. 'Why is he still on the employee list, then?'

'Month's notice,' said the manager. 'We paid him a month's notice. He'd been here long enough for that. I knew as soon as he said he was going, he wouldn't be back in, and he hadn't been. We're still paying him a notice. That was our side of the contract. I could turn around and go after it, but to be honest, he's not worth it, not worth causing all the hassle. I've got plenty enough to do.'

'You say his kids are at Newcastle?'

'Yes,' said the manager. 'Tommy believed in family. Tommy believed in a lot of things. Don't get me wrong. Tommy was a reasonable guy if things were going his way. Before things kicked off and he couldn't get his time to go down to Newcastle, he would tell me about his kids, how he loved them, about how Christmas was for families. "Christmas was a time that was unique," Tommy said. I remember it. It was almost like a speech. I had stood there with a couple of others. I think Mandy from accounts was there. He went on for five minutes about what he would do at Christmas with the kids. How it was important for this time off, how the family bonded because of this, even if there were other troubles going on.'

'Do you know why he's up here and his kids are down there? Is he estranged from his wife or partner?'

'Partner,' said the manager. 'I don't quite know how well they get on, but there must be some degree of cooperation. After all, he went down to see the kids.'

'It's possible that Tommy could have headed back to Newcastle,' said Macleod.

'I think so. Haven't seen Tommy since the day he left here. I know John, down in the chilled foods department, John said that he'd seen him out in the pub. Tommy had said hello. John and him didn't really speak that much, so it wasn't unusual to get nothing from him. Just a quick hello and how do you do? Given the way he left here, I wouldn't go looking for him.'

'That's understandable. I need to get hold of his wife, though, or partner, or whoever she is. I need to get hold of Tommy,' said Macleod.

'If he's having problems,' said Ross, 'we could ask for social services.'

'When do you need to get a hold of him by?' asked the store manager. 'I can go into the records, see if we have anything, but to be totally honest, he had an address up here. His family, his business beyond that, wasn't any concern of ours. Other than asking for the leave, we don't need to know anything else.'

'I appreciate that, sir, but if you could look, I would be much obliged to you.'

The man stood up and left the room. Macleod turned to Ross. 'I think he's fitting a profile.'

Ross wasn't aware that any profile had been produced. 'What do you mean?' asked Ross.

'Think about it. Whoever is doing this, it's one of two bets. They're either some nut job who on seeing a computer game, wants to copy it and carry it out in real life. How many of those come to fruition? None. Next to none. They really are one-offs. Think about it from the other side,' said Macleod.

'You mean from someone with a semi-rational mind?' said Ross.

'Yes, exactly. Imagine you hold firm beliefs about Christmas,' said Macleod. 'Imagine that you prize it as being one of the

184

most important things. They always say it's the day when kids' wishes come true. Forget the religious side and make it more about the wonderful Santa Claus side,' said Macleod.

'You're thinking we could look at someone who sees that dream brought down,' said Ross.

'Exactly. Someone so wound up in it he sees that day, that time is what keeps the family together. It's what builds them up. It's what gives the glue for the following year.'

'Then you get told you can't have it,' said Ross. 'Then you get told that all that matters is you coming in and doing the work and leaving. You'd have to be really strong on it. You'd have to be.'

'Very dedicated to the cause too,' said the Macleod. 'Maybe a touch unstable with it, but then again, if you go out murdering people, there's usually a touch of instability there. Even if you're incredibly rational in your own way.'

The manager of the store came back in, shaking his head. 'I'm afraid I have nothing. No details beyond. I'm sorry. Maybe you could try social services. I know there were issues.'

'Sit down a moment,' said Macleod, and saw the manager's face. 'I know you're in a rush. I know you need to get back out there and wrap the store up, but please give me five minutes.' The man sat down.

'Tommy—what do you know of his background beyond Newcastle.'

'Tommy used to be in the services, military. He's got several tattoos up his arm and he served in different places. He also came from a big family. I remember he talked about them. His father left them all, and I think his mother raised them. He was big on family. Never got over his father. One of the few people I remember he talked with real spite about. He also used to talk a lot about politics.'

'Was he very passionate on these beliefs?' asked Macleod.

'He was going to join the union. He wanted to be a union rep at one point. God forgive me. He's the last person I would want on the planet to be a union rep. On and on he'd go. He'd be committed to the mass, committed to the core. He's everything you wouldn't want as a store manager or a union rep. There'd be no compromise.

'I think that's what really got me about Tommy. When he was debating things, or he was thinking things over in his mind, when he got to the answer, that was it. It was black and white. On a couple of political issues we talked about on the rare occasion in the early days, you couldn't sway him and action needed to be taken. I don't know; he took action sometimes. I know he went out and protested with placards for events in the Middle East. Incredibly passionate about his beliefs,' said the manager. 'Almost dogmatic when he made up his mind. Also prepared to commit to the cause. Whatever he saw that as being.'

'Let me understand this,' said Macleod. 'He had also been in the military. Had he seen active service?'

'Oh, yes. He told me a few times about some rather bad incidents, times he had to kill people.'

'When he did that, how was he talking about them?'

'Well, at first it took me by surprise,' said the manager. 'You see, he was quite cold, quite clinical about it. It was a job. It's what you had to do. I was expecting a lot more regret, but it wasn't there. He said to me it was regrettable that they had to be killed, but at the end of the day, that's what made the situation work. He didn't seem to have any qualms about having to carry it out. I guess if you're in the military, maybe that's the way you think. Don't know, never having been a soldier.'

'I'm not sure all the military think anything like that,' said Macleod, 'but you've been very helpful. Thank you.'

The manager stood up and went to walk away. Then he turned back, 'Can I expect you to be out of here by five? Maybe six, so I can close up.'

Macleod nodded. 'I don't think there's anything else you can help us with.'

As the manager left, Ross turned to Macleod. 'What are you thinking?'

'Thomas Wilson fits the bill,' said Macleod, 'but we don't even know if he's still here. We don't know where he is. If he does fit the bill and if it is him, I'm struggling to know how we get to him. I need to know everything we can about him.' Macleod picked up his mobile phone. 'I'm about to do probably the most difficult task I've ever done in my police service.'

Ross raised an eyebrow. 'Catch Thomas Wilson? Really?'

'No,' said Macleod. 'I'm going to get a hold of Social Services at close to five o'clock on Christmas Eve. How many of them do you think are going to be kicking about?'

'Well, we're here. Maybe they've got a case or something.'

'Come on, Ross. Unless you must be here, you won't be here.'

Macleod picked up his phone while Ross gathered together all the paperwork and put it back in the small bag he'd brought it in. Within a minute, he could hear Macleod thunder down the phone.

'Will you find me somebody who can? I don't care. This is Detective Chief Inspector Macleod. I need to speak to someone who knows. . . . I don't care if they're in the middle of a Christmas party. . . . I don't care if they've just headed off somewhere. You get them on a phone for me. You might be about to leave the office. I'm here. I'm on a case, and I'm trying to stop someone from dying tonight. Sort it out. I'd hate for the inquiry to come through and you be the problem. You be the reason we didn't get to someone.'

Ross didn't dare look at Macleod. Part of him was laughing. Seoras could kick-off when he wanted to. He had that mannerism about him. He could be brisk with people, but he was also delicate. Whoever had answered the phone had obviously told him he had to be joking. Didn't he know it was Christmas?

As Ross zipped up his bag, all his papers tucked away, he had a hollow feeling in his stomach. He'd hoped they'd come here, find someone guilty, and then they could pick them up. That would be it, and he'd be back with Angus and the little one for Christmas. Instead, it felt like it was going to be a long night.

# Chapter 22

Hope stood at the edge of a large room with disco music and flashing lights. The constant thump, thump, thump of the beat was annoying her. She couldn't hear anything, and she was sweating. In front of her on the dance floor, people were gyrating rather drunkenly.

Hope could remember the days when she used to go clubbing, dressed in as little as some others who were out on the floor. She couldn't remember if they were good or bad times. You would've had the high of being there, and then the next morning you'd have felt like hell.

These days she went out with John. They'd have a meal, they'd go to the cinema, or the theatre, or they'd go to some sports event. They didn't go to clubs anymore. Was that because she was getting old? Besides, she'd have rather slow-danced with John. He couldn't really do any other sort of dance.

She turned and looked at Susan Cunningham beside her. Susan had taken her jacket off, such was the heat of the place, and was drinking a glass of water. The pair of them were the only ones not either swilling down a large amount of alcohol, or up gyrating on the floor. Some people were shouting at each other, arms wrapped around shoulders, congratulating each other about something. A few were snogging, as they said, and she watched as they were almost tearing the mouths off each other. She looked at Susan and mouthed, 'We need to go.'

Susan shook her head, and she pointed out towards Donna, the butcher's daughter. She was gyrating in a lewd fashion with two younger men. Hope couldn't see where their hands were, but from time to time they would dance in a rather— what they probably thought was sexy—fashion. From Hope's point of view, it was grotesque. However, Donna was keeping the men interested.

One of them was called Jason. Black-haired, around about six feet. He could nearly come eye to eye with Hope. He had placed several kisses on Donna, and she'd turned back and opened her mouth in a rather sloppy fest that Hope didn't really want to watch. As the music continued, hands went to places that they really shouldn't be, and Hope got more agitated. Somewhere there was a killer out there tonight. Two, in fact. At least that's what the team thought. Here they were just standing, looking at some drunk people fondling each other.

The owner of the butcher shop came up to Hope, imploring her again to come and have a drink with him. She shook her head and then turned back to Susan to complain, but her colleague wasn't there. She was off across the room, staring at Donna from a different angle, and then she was talking to someone. A woman of maybe twenty-five.

*How could she hear anything?* thought Hope, and saw the woman was talking directly into Susan's ear, almost shouting into it from no distance at all. Susan came back over towards

Hope, indicated she needed to bend down, and when Hope did so, shouted into her ear.

'They think it's going to kick off. Donna teased too many of them. Looks like some boys are going to come to fisticuffs. There's been a few arguments already.'

Susan also pointed over towards Emma. She was sitting at a table rather quietly. Donna's sister seemed uninterested in what Donna was doing, and Hope watched as the woman got up and disappeared out to where the cloak rooms were. She then walked around the room for a moment before sitting down again.

Meanwhile, there was some pushing and shoving on the floor. Hope watched as Jason seemed to grab Donna for himself and then pushed away one of the other lads. Donna said something to him. He reacted badly, walked over to a table, picked up a pint, and drank a good half of it before putting the glass rather loudly back down.

Donna came towards him, wrapping her arms around him, but he shrugged her off. Then he turned and pushed one of the other boys. Hope went to react, but Susan put her hand across, shaking her head. She wanted it to play out, but Susan wasn't looking at the fight. She was looking around the room.

Hope couldn't clock what she was looking at, and the music was too loud to ask. Instead, she saw Jason walk over to his coat, take something, then march over to one of the boys. Donna stepped in front of him, spoke with him for a moment, and then he disappeared.

Hope wondered what he was doing. What had he taken from his coat? Did he have a knife? Was this part of what it was? Was there a costume elsewhere? Hope could feel Susan reach for her, but strode across the dance floor anyway and straight out through the door that Jason had taken.

She looked along the carpeted hallway and noticed that one door at the end was swinging. She raced down to it and saw it was the men's toilet. *Was he going in there to change? Is that where he had his outfit? Had he just picked up his weapon and now he was heading for an outfit?*

Hope pushed open the doors, looked inside, and saw a young lad at a urinal, urinating into it with his back to her. She ignored him, and instead, looked at the cubicles and saw that one had its door closed. She bent down and saw a pair of smart shoes, just like Jason was wearing.

'Jason,' said Hope, probably too loudly. She was now in a quieter room without the deafeningly loud music. 'Jason, I need you to come out of the cubicle.'

'What the hell, lady? I'm having a piss,' said the urinating man.

'Finish up and get out,' said Hope.

The boy zipped himself up, walked past Hope, and then stopped, looking at her. 'Seriously, Jason, you've pulled this one?'

'Out!' yelled Hope. The young man opened the door of the toilets and left as Hope banged on the cubicle. 'I know you're in there. I hope you're unarmed. You don't have to go through with this. You realise that, don't you? It's not worth it. You open the door,' said Hope.

There was no response from the other side. She crouched again quickly. The shoes were sitting exactly where they were before. Hope was going to look over the top, but the cubicle was high. She didn't have time for this. She stepped forward and planted an almighty boot where she thought the hinge of the lock would be. It wasn't strong, and the door flew open.

Sitting on the toilet was Jason. He was slumped, a needle lying on his lap, his arm tied up with a tourniquet. He had clearly injected himself with something.

'Jason, Jason,' said Hope, slapping his face. She watched, and he was still breathing. She pulled out her phone. There was no signal. *Damn it*, she thought.

Hope turned and ran back towards the room where the loud music was. As she bolted through the door, Donna was still in the middle, dancing away, but she couldn't see Susan. She needed Susan. She needed to get help for the boy.

Then all the lights went out. The music switched off. It was like a power cut, except there were lights outside the building. Through the curtains she could see the faint lights of town, but the room was flooded in darkness.

'Oh,' said someone. 'Spooky. It's Christmas, not Halloween.'

A light came on and illuminated Donna. It was a spotlight from the ceiling. As Hope looked, she could see Donna, but someone had an arm around her throat. It was a slender arm, but the light was shining in such a way that at first, she couldn't make out the figure behind, and then she saw it.

The person had a mask on with red eyes. It wasn't particularly glamorous. The mask's image was unfamiliar, but the red eyes told Hope all she needed to know. It was the Badalisc. It was going down right now. Jason was fighting for his life in the toilet while here, someone was about to attack Donna.

'Nobody moves or she's dead,' said a female voice from inside the Badalisc head. Her hand reached down and pulled up Donna's dress. It went past the green underwear she was wearing and up to expose her bare belly. The hand stopped rising once the belly was exposed.

'It's in there. It's in there. This slut's got a child. A child is in there and it belongs to him.'

The Badalisc was suddenly pointing with a human hand at one of the young men. He seemed rather drunk, his face bizarre. There were shouts, there was some laughter, but Hope cried out, 'No, don't do it. You can't do it.'

Other people screamed. Hope was too far away, and a hand of the Badalisc disappeared behind the figure into the shadows.

'He's married,' shouted the Badalisc. 'He's married, and you had him. Homewrecker! You'll destroy the business! You'll bring it down on all of us.'

The butcher shouted, screaming, 'Emma, don't. No,' as he recognised his own daughter's voice, about to attack her own sister.

'With this knife, I'll cut it out. With this knife, you'll pay for what you've done.'

Hope could see the Badalisc reach behind it, seeking within its clothing for something. The knife that would be there. Hope ran, but the Badalisc kept reaching with its arm, fumbling, and then it spun round.

The light had been focused on Donna, but as the Badalisc turned and pulled Donna with it, it moved slightly out of the spotlight. The unblocked light then spread to behind where the Badalisc had been standing. Holding a knife in her right hand was Susan Cunningham.

'Don't. No, no.'

The Badalisc let go of Donna, who choking, fell to the floor. Hope ran over, snatched the arm of the Badalisc, driving it up behind its back and slapped cuffs on it. Susan Cunningham gave her a smile.

'Don't take this the wrong way,' said Hope. 'Well done, but I've got somebody dying from a drugs overdose in the toilet.

Can you get a signal?'

Susan pulled out her phone. 'No,' she said, 'I'll get downstairs. They'll have a phone.'

She raced off as quick as she could while Hope took off the mask of the Badalisc. Across the room, the butcher was crying, stumbling towards his older daughter, putting his arms around Donna. Emma was yelling at him, crying out that she deserved nothing, that all she deserved was to be cut up. She had killed Christmas. She had destroyed what was.

Hope looked around her, trying to find anyone that was vaguely sober. It was two minutes before Susan Cunningham came back and Hope sent her out towards the toilet. Susan worked as best as she could while Hope maintained her grip on Emma. The woman was someone she couldn't leave alone.

Paramedics arrived and Susan and Hope took Emma downstairs to a police car that they'd called for. The two constables would take her in for processing and they'd talk to her later. Right now, they needed to contact Macleod and find out if the other killer had been found.

Hope would need to see where it was best to deploy herself. Maybe Emma would tell them something; maybe she wouldn't. Meanwhile, the party upstairs had collapsed, and Hope knew she would need statements from the people who had been there.

More constables had arrived, and she organised the people. Taking statements from drunk people was never easy. Would enough of them be sober to actually recall what had happened? Some were still laughing and joking, but Hope looked over at a man who'd seen his business do as well as it could that year. Now, on Christmas Eve, he was sitting bereft. One daughter shamed, and the other being held for attempted murder. Sitting in the arms of John in front of the fire seemed a lot more palatable than the mess she'd encountered tonight. She turned to look at Susan Cunningham, but the woman smiled back at her.

'One to go!'

# Chapter 23

Clarissa parked the little green sports car and raced to the edge of the superstore, looking for Macleod. She grabbed hold of one of the security guards. They told her the 'flipping' policeman was still in there. He would have to close the place up soon. Clarissa ignored him, made her way through, and found Macleod and Ross in a room with an irate-looking store manager.

'He said he'd be out of here.'

'We'll be going soon,' said Ross quietly to the man. In the other corner, Macleod was on the phone.

'I don't give two hoots. You need to call them all, all of them, and call me right back. I need to speak to them. I need to find Thomas Wilson. This is a murder inquiry. I'm trying to prevent one. I don't care if it is Christmas.'

Clarissa walked over to Ross. 'Where are we at?'

'Hope and Susan have found the Badalisc. They've stopped it.'

'Good,' said Clarissa. 'One more and I can go home.'

'It's the social services down in Newcastle he's on to. The boss thinks he's got somebody. He thinks he's got someone who fits the bill. A Thomas Wilson. The trouble is trying to find out about him. He used to work here, left about a month or so ago, blaming it all on Christmas, blaming it all on not getting to Newcastle. Incredibly strong-minded individual, very big on his beliefs. Felt that if something was right, you did it. Also, ex-military capable of killing, capable of . . .'

Clarissa's face was falling, 'Capable of hiding,' she said. 'Capable of making sure that we don't find him until it's too late.'

'We're not sure we're going to trace him to a location. Apparently, he's quite a big family man, but he couldn't get to see his kids this Christmas. Saw that as a major part of it.'

'He's playing Santa. He's playing the main individual in all of this. No wonder he's fitting the bill,' said Clarissa.

Clarissa strode over to Macleod. He had paused briefly, no longer arguing with the other end of the call.

'What do you want me to do?' she asked him.

'Ross bring you up to speed?'

'Yes.'

'I need to know where he's going to do it. If it's him, where is he going to do it. I'm trying to get any information I can from Newcastle and see if I can build up a picture, but he was here. See if you can find a grudge. See if you can find someone he would think deserved to die over Christmas.'

Clarissa nodded her head and turned away. *How is that a thing?* she asked herself. *How am I even asking that? How is this guy got so worked up that he's prepared to kill somebody over not running Christmas right? He must have a screw loose. There must be something wrong with him.* Then she stopped. 'Don't,' she said out loud. 'This is logical to him. This is logical.'

She turned and walked over to the store manager, who was hopping on his feet.

'How many of the staff are left?' she asked.

'One or two,' he said, 'I just need to close the store up.'

'Any of them know Tommy really well? Any of them really talk to him?'

'Most of us still here are management. Tommy didn't talk to us. Not about anything serious. You could try the security guy. He talks to everyone.'

Clarissa nodded and marched outside, finding the security guard standing by the door.

'DS Clarissa Urquhart,' she said, pulling out a warrant card. 'Are you on for the rest of the night?'

'Got the Christmas watch,' he said. 'But I've got a little room and I'll have some Christmas pudding and a little Turkey dinner thing I've made up. Then I'll sit and watch some comedy and do my rounds whenever, because let's face it, nobody's going to come in here to nick anything. I'm happy enough,' he said. 'But I just want to get settled in. It's pretty cold out here.'

'You're not kidding,' said Clarissa. She threw her shawl around herself again, as the snow started to fall.

'Quite picturesque, though,' said the man. 'I guess it's the right thing, you know, snow at Christmas and that.'

'Snow's nice when you're looking out a window,' said Clarissa, 'with a big fire beside you and some man to cuddle up to you.'

For a moment, the man looked a little perturbed. Clarissa shook her head.

'I wasn't suggesting that you and I get intimate. I've got a man at home, a husband,' she said. 'It's just I'd rather be there.' The man laughed for a moment, and then Clarissa put on her more serious face. 'I was speaking to the boss inside. He said that you might know something about Thomas Wilson.'

'Tommy,' said the security guard. 'We used to natter a bit. I'm ex-military as well.'

'Right, so you had something in common then. Did he talk much about life in general?'

'Tommy always talked. Tommy always had an agenda. I listened a lot, you know. Tommy was fine. He was okay, but you took him in small doses. Everybody has something to blame. I tell you something, see, if you were the Prime Minister coming up here for a visit or something, you wouldn't have Tommy near you in front of the cameras. He'd hit you with everything that was wrong about the UK, Scotland, everything.'

Clarissa gave a small chortle. 'Did he have anyone in the local area he was particularly angry about?'

'Oh, he could complain about everyone in the local area. Town planning, everything. Services too. Things weren't right. Because he was estranged from his wife, Tommy had wanted to get a home up here with them. But they lived in Newcastle. She wasn't going to move up anyway, but he didn't blame it on her.

'He blamed that on the council not giving them the house because if they had given him a pleasant house and that, she'd have enjoyed that and she'd have come up. They'd have got back together and paradise would have happened.

'That was Tommy. Tommy could always blame somebody who wasn't close to him. His wife, Laura, well, she wasn't his wife—she was his partner. They never quite managed to marry, though he had three kids with her. Laura, from what I can gather, probably saw it best to keep Tommy at a distance. Although I think she was okay with him coming down. I think she could see the slightly darker side he had. Probably wanted to protect the kids from that. He said often she was very strict about what Tommy could and couldn't do with them. He wasn't allowed to talk politics around them or anything like that.'

'I don't think anybody should talk politics around kids, bad enough they speak it around me,' said Clarissa. She gave a little smile and stamped her feet in the cold.

'Do you ever think he could harm anyone? Was there anyone he had that nastier side aimed towards?'

'Tommy got into a few scraps in the pubs over politics. Politics was the big one. There was an article in the paper two months back that got his bug up. It was about the housing and there was an issue around the provost. I don't quite recall why the provost was responsible. In fact, I think I remember thinking to myself, *How is the provost responsible for this?* But Tommy was blaming him.

'Anyway, Tommy went to see him when he was doing one of his visits. It was a local school and a massive row. I think the provost may have put a . . . well, he didn't quite put a restraining order on him, but if any of the provost's people seen him, they would keep Tommy away. He wasn't welcome certainly at the offices when Tommy was trying to get after him. In fact, I remember him saying to me that the bastard had cut all ties with him, wouldn't speak to him. That's the words he used. Sorry, I try not to use that language around ladies.'

Clarissa gave a nod. She appreciated the thought of not using such language around her, but in truth, she probably used much worse on a fairly frequent basis.

'How much did he hate the provost?' asked Clarissa. 'And please don't hold back, I need to know his exact feelings.'

'I didn't hear him speak more ill of anyone else,' said the man. 'Would he have done anything to him? I can't say. Tommy was not an open book. There were parts of Tommy that were dark. I didn't go to those places. I'm running security here. When Tommy's about, he talks to you. But I'm not here to exorcise his demons or to indeed bring on any new ones. So please, I'm not saying he would harm the provost, but I'm not saying he wouldn't. I'm just saying that the provost was the one that was bugging him the last I knew him.'

'That's very helpful,' said Clarissa. 'Have a good night. I'll try to chivvy my boss along and get you in the warm soon.'

'Thank you,' said the man. 'Merry Christmas.'

'Let's hope so,' said Clarissa. She walked back inside the superstore to find Macleod and Ross heading for the exit.

'How goes it?' she asked.

'I finally got through, got to talk to Tommy's partner.'

'Laura?' said Clarissa.

Macleod was stunned for a moment. 'How did you—never mind. Anyway, she said that he called a while back, said that he couldn't be there and told the kids he couldn't make it. He's not gone down to Newcastle.'

'That means he could still be about. I just spoke outside to the security guard,' said Clarissa. 'Tommy was very political. Someone who was forthright in his views. Apparently, he could really go down the line when he thought something was wrong.'

'Well, yes,' said Macleod. 'That's why I think it's him.'

'His current thing before he left was the provost. Something about housing. He'd had a couple of bust-ups with the provost. The provost seems to be a link in.'

'Good work,' said Macleod. 'Right, let's try the provost's

office.'

'There's not going to be anybody there, is there?' said Clarissa.

Macleod was dialling a number. 'Maybe not. Maybe I need to get hold of someone.'

Macleod hung on the phone for thirty seconds until he got the message saying that the provost's office was closed and to have a happy Christmas. There was a beep, and he left a message saying that he was to be contacted as soon as possible if anyone picked this up.

'No one there,' he said. 'No one there.'

'Right then, where else do we go?'

'You could try the desk sergeant,' said Ross. 'He usually knows everything that's going on in town. He probably knows where the provost is.'

'Good idea,' said Macleod. They stepped outside into the snow, Clarissa and Ross shivering as Macleod placed a call. Behind them, the doors of the superstore were being locked up, and the manager tapped Macleod on the shoulder as he left.

'Thanks for your assistance,' said Macleod.

'Merry Christmas,' said the man back to him.

'Merry Christmas. Bye.' And then the phone was picked up by the desk sergeant. 'Anderson,' said Macleod. 'Tell me, do you know anything about where the provost is tonight?'

'The provost? Are you joking?'

'It's Macleod; do I normally joke?'

'No, sir,' said Anderson. 'The provost is going to be at the big do.'

'The big do,' said Macleod. 'Remind me.'

Anything of note seemed to fly past Macleod. If it was a

social gathering, if it was some sort of celebration, Macleod's mind always switched off to it. He might have known it was going on, but he could never recall the times or the places.

'Starting at half-six tonight. Extravaganza, the big stage in the middle of town, sir. McTavish is back on again. It's the same one where they had the Krampus trying to take people out, but don't worry, we've got plenty of people about. There's going to be a celebration.'

'What sort of thing is happening at it?'

'Oh, they got the pipers, they've got dancing, et cetera, and of course, Christmas Eve, so Santa's got to make an appearance.'

Macleod's blood ran cold. 'When is Santa doing his appearance?'

'I don't know. It's not going on too late. I mean, they want people to get home to sort out Christmas presents, get the kids back to bed. I'd imagine if the kiddies are there, oh, it's got to be the next half hour an hour before Santa gets there, wouldn't you? The noise can already be heard from the station.'

Macleod said thanks and closed down the call. He turned his head. He could hear the deep sound of a bass beat. It was coming from a fair distance. There was a beam of light shining up into the sky, then another.

'Well?' asked Clarissa.

'Over there,' said Macleod. 'The big stage in town. The provost is going to be there; apparently. Santa is paying a visit.'

Macleod looked over at Clarissa. She looked at Ross, the three of them for a moment realising the scene was set. 'The car,' said Macleod. 'The car.'

'I've got mine,' said Clarissa. 'Get yourself in. You follow with yours, Ross,' said Clarissa. 'Let's go.'

Macleod ran with Clarissa over to the little green sports car and they both jumped in. The snow fell heavily as she spun the wheel, hurrying out onto the link road.

'Go,' said Macleod. 'Go, go.'

'I'm going, Seoras. Shut up!'

His hands were sitting in front of him, his knuckle's white as he held onto the dash.

*I got out of the murder squad for this very reason, because of the horror. This is the last hurrah,* she told herself. *'One last time. There'll be no more after this.*

# Chapter 24

'Watch the road,' shouted Macleod.

Clarissa ignored him, swinging her little green car past first one car, then another. Was she strictly on the speed limit? Well, frankly, she couldn't care less. They had to get there, had to warn people of what was going on. Besides, Macleod was only complaining because he was trying to use the phone at the same time.

'Hope,' said Macleod, catching his breath as Clarissa swung past another car, 'you need to get to the big stage in town. I think that's where it's going down. Thomas Wilson is our suspect.'

'Who's Thomas Wilson?' asked Hope.

'Worked in the superstore in town. Ross and I have just been there. Trust me, I'm not going to go into it now, but I think he's our target.'

'What's he going to do, and where?'

'I believe he's making for the big stage in town. He'll be dressed as Santa Claus. Father Christmas is making an appearance. It seems he had some sort of bugbear with the provost. I think he's looking to take him out.'

'Okay,' said Hope. 'I'm on my way now. I'm bringing Susan

with me. I'm going to leave the constables in charge of clearing up behind us.'

'Good idea. All hands to the pump!'

Macleod closed the call before informing Patterson at the station. The little green car seemed to weave in and out, narrowly missing many objects on the way into town. Macleod put his head down to make his phone calls. Beside him, Clarissa didn't flinch, her eyes focused on the road ahead.

The car had been fixed up by Macleod, and boy, had he done a good job on it. *It flew*, she thought. The vehicle was a part of her, and she wondered if any of them ever thought of her without it. Frank had mentioned getting a more sensible car, and that had been put to bed, very quickly. If you accepted Clarissa, you accepted sitting in the passenger seat of her little baby.

It wasn't long before they reached a point at which they couldn't get in any closer with the car. She parked up, Macleod already jumping out. Clarissa locked the car behind her. She wasn't entirely happy with where it was because of the crowds of people around, but needs must. Macleod was trying to push his way through.

'This is Detective Chief Inspector Macleod. Make way, I need to get through to the stage. I need to get through to the stage.'

It was hard going. Many people weren't happy to let him through. A view of the stage was difficult to procure. The music was loud. Many were staring up at the light show that was going on.

'Shift your arse,' shouted Clarissa from behind Macleod. 'Chief Inspector coming through. I said, shift your arse. You.' Somebody got a dig in the ribs and shifted.

'Oi,' said the man, and tried to push back.

'You do that, sunshine, and you'll end up with a night in the cells. Now get your arse moving.'

Macleod wasn't sure that this was the correct etiquette, but it didn't matter anymore. The music went quiet and Macleod stopped for a moment to look up towards the stage. Clarissa didn't stop, instead pushing a path through, Macleod slowly walking in her wake, but as he looked on stage, he saw McTavish making an announcement.

The little man was out in his tartan trews and waistcoat, bubbling, wishing everyone Merry Christmas and telling them to shout ho, ho, ho! 'Santa Claus is Coming to Town' was now blaring over the speakers. Macleod tried to phone, tried to tell someone, but he couldn't be heard.

He went up behind Clarissa, shouting into her ear. 'You've got to get on that stage now. We've got to get on.'

His phone rang. He tried to answer it and thought he could make out Hope. She was yelling something about not being there. Was he close?

He closed the call. He couldn't make himself heard to her or her be heard by him. It was down to him. He followed in Clarissa's wake, the crowd incredibly deep, all fixated on the stage until someone's elbow shoved into his side.

Macleod looked up. He was only three people from the line of bouncers around the stage, Clarissa brushing aside the last of the public. Santa was strolling on to the stage, a sack over his shoulder, and there beside McTavish was the provost, standing and applauding, welcoming him. Macleod saw the provost's face, and it went into a face of horror. He wasn't a tall man, but he was a plump man, and the fatty jowls on the provost's face sunk. Macleod saw Santa was holding a gun. McTavish backed away, backpedalling.

Meanwhile, the bouncers were looking at a perturbed audience, and Clarissa was climbing the fence to get up to the stage. Three of them had now stepped towards her, one receiving a kick to the face for his troubles, the other trying to push her back.

'DS Urquhart, get the hell out of the way. There's a man with a gun on the stage.'

Macleod tried to climb up onto the metal fencing that ran around the stage, and he shoved his warrant card in the face of one of the bouncers. He pointed to the stage, the man turning round.

Meanwhile, on the stage, Santa had thrown a sack over the provost, McTavish no longer there. The provost was then knocked to the ground, and Santa tied him up inside the sack. Santa stood at least six feet four and didn't look like the fat, jolly man on all the Christmas cards. This man was a giant, a brute, and he slung the provost over his shoulder in the sack. A couple of bouncers tried to get onto the stage, but a gun was pointed at them, and they backed away.

As Macleod stepped up towards the stage, a terrible thought went through his mind. Somebody had said to win the game, Santa emptied someone out of the sack, down the chimney. Macleod looked at the backdrop.

The stage had a backdrop of houses, and there was an enormous chimney coming out of one. It even had a smoking effect. The windows of the house were lit like one of those plastic Christmas sets which you put on your windowsill that showed that Christmas was here. The snow lying all around, the warmth of inside, the chimney showing the fire, and Santa landing on the roof. Except, Santa now was climbing up the house.

The houses were just a façade around steel framing which allowed Santa to climb towards the fake chimney. Clarissa was hopping onto the stage, and a constable ran on from the side.

'Take cover,' shouted Macleod at Clarissa. 'Take cover!'

He could see she was in that mood. During the time he'd worked with her, he had thought her a cross between someone who was reckless and incredibly determined. Someone was about to die. Despite all she'd been through, Clarissa was going to rescue them. He knew it. He wouldn't be able to stop her.

Santa waved the gun around and then took a shot down towards the stage. The constable dived to one side, crawling off the stage, but Clarissa ran towards the houses, putting herself flat against them. Santa seemed to ignore her, putting his gun away and climbing up the structure.

The structure was of rectangular construction, a long tube, four posts with criss-crosses in-between. You might fit a rather large person down the middle with just room for a little more. It wasn't a chimney designed for proper use. It was fake. Looking at the stage, all you saw was a chimney rising. Santa was now climbing on the metal bars that supported the structure at the back, but the crowd could see him climb. They were fascinated, like Macleod was, entranced by the horror show going on before them.

He could see Clarissa had started to climb too. Her tartan trews and shawl blowing in the wind. Santa took his gun out again, firing down towards Clarissa. Macleod looked, and she wasn't there. Where'd she gone?

He raced over to the structure. Santa had resumed climbing. Macleod reached the bottom of the structure, but there was no way he could climb up in time. He looked up at the snowflakes falling down on his face, and saw the red figure taking the sack off its shoulder. Santa was turning now, facing the crowd, laughing.

'Ho, ho, ho.'

The crowd had descended into a deathly hush. This is what Thomas Wilson wanted. This was the game. In reality, he was about to throw the provost down a fake chimney. Everyone would be watching, everyone would see. Then Tommy will probably calmly climb down and explain to everyone what he'd done and why he'd done it. Was he expecting everyone to then become festive?

*This is madness*, thought Macleod. *Madness. What had driven the man to it? Had it been the breakup of his family? Was it not being able to get to see his kids? Had it been the stress he'd endured out with the military?*

Macleod didn't know, but what could he do? Santa could now wrap his legs around part of the structure. The sack was off his back, and he was starting to tip the provost out. The provost didn't know where he had been tipped from. Suddenly let loose from hanging in a sack, his legs hit the top of the structure. His arm shot out, and he was stuck right at the top. For some reason, the provost wasn't falling.

He had caught on something. Tommy tried to push him, but the provost didn't go down. Santa looked over, pushing the provost to one side, who was suddenly hanging onto one side of the chimney, his legs wrapped around it, his arms too.

White fear showed on the provost's face. Macleod looked up, saw Clarissa suddenly climbing up beside the provost. Tommy took out his gun. Before he could point it again at Clarissa, she was shaking the man's hand. Was she holding on tight? Would

211

he overpower her? He was surely stronger than her. Macleod shook the structure, putting a shoulder to it, back and forward as he looked up. Santa wavered for a second, then he slipped. The gun fell to one side, and Santa tipped forward.

Some of the bolts that had clearly been undone for part of the structure below Santa, Clarissa, and the provost collapsed. It tilted to one side and Santa tipped forward, sailing through the air, crashing down headfirst on the stage. The top half of the chimney structure broke off into the crowd. It looked like the chimney had cracked in half, part of it suddenly leaning off at an acute angle. Clarissa dropped, but caught onto part of the structure. Together, Clarissa and the provost hung on, stopping it from tipping over completely at the top.

'Seoras,' she screamed. 'Someone, someone.'

Macleod was in shock. Six feet away from him, the battered corpse of Tommy Wilson lay motionless, blood pouring across the stage. Above him, his sergeant was screaming. Suddenly beside him, a figure began climbing, her red hair blowing in the wind in a familiar ponytail. Alongside her, a blonde figure with another ponytail climbed too. Macleod stood frozen as the two figures ran up at incredible speed, climbing for all they were worth. The chimney was tipping. The section that had broken off was about to keel over. Clarissa would go—the provost, also.

Macleod shouted at others who were now coming onto the stage to step back, to get clear. The chimney tipped. He looked up to see Clarissa let go, as did the provost. The provost grabbed the pipe at the top and was hanging on, but Clarissa was falling. She dropped some three feet before a hand snatched her. She swung left and right, and a second hand grabbed her.

There was a course of expletives. Macleod had never heard her swear so much, and then he saw her hands reach out and grab hold of the metal structure, wrapping herself around it.

The chimney had toppled, crashing into part of the stage which had collapsed, the rest of the metal falling away to the rear. People were running onto the stage now, medics approaching Tommy Wilson, but Macleod knew it was pointless. Others helped bring Clarissa down along with the provost. Macleod just sat on the stage. Before him was a dead man, his questions unanswered. What had driven him to it? What had made the man do it?

Macleod waited, ready to hear the voice of the man in the grey monk's habit. Would he chastise him? He'd see Tommy Wilson was dead. He would tease him for it. He would tell him it was his fault as the snow fell thickly on his shoulders and covered the stage.

Macleod heard nothing. There was no grey-hooded figure. A pair of arms were flung round Macleod. It was Hope. Clarissa put another arm around him. Susan joined in too. He then looked up to see Ross standing, smiling at all of them. As the crowd noise grew, people asking what had gone on, their terrified silence breaking into desperate explanation, the team took a moment.

They were all alive, and they'd done it. The view to Macleod's right, of the man they were now clearing up from the stage, meant he didn't feel like celebrating. In fact, he would have to shake the snow off himself. It was time to go back to work, and it would be a long night. Although it was over, there was clearing up to do. It looked like they were spending Christmas at the station.

# Chapter 25

Y ou didn't have to come in,' said Macleod, 'but I'm glad you did.' He put his arms around Jane as she entered the office.

'What was I meant to do?' she said. 'Sit at home with my turkey? You were going to be in here. The least I could do was come in and try to make sure you were all fed, at least. I mean, have you eaten anything?'

'We had breakfast. We still have officers out doing their normal shift. The station still runs.'

'I have organised a little something,' said Jane. 'I said that you guys would be still here.'

'How did you ever get sway in this place?'

Jane kissed him on the cheek. 'I told them I was working for a certain Detective Chief Inspector.'

'Then you think I have sway?'

'I told them I was his partner. I was the one that looked after him.'

'What did they say to that?'

"God bless you,' they said; 'you could do with all the help you can get."

Macleod laughed, and Jane hugged him tight. She took out

214

some mistletoe and held it up over him.

'I want my Christmas kiss, Seoras. I want a Christmas morning together in a warm bed. But it'll have to be Christmas night,' she said. She kissed him deeply, and when she broke off, she looked at him. 'I just thanked God this morning you were all okay.'

'As did I,' he said, 'as did I.'

'We need to go downstairs,' said Jane. 'I got the canteen to do Christmas dinner for your lot. We're going to bring it up, you and me.'

'So, I've got to work?' said Macleod.

Jane smacked his backside. 'You work for me to the day you die,' she said. 'Come on.' She turned and walked towards the door. Macleod stopped, looking over to the corner.

'Is he still here?' asked Jane. 'Still giving you grief?'

'No,' said Macleod, 'he's not. Last night he just disappeared. I keep waiting for him to come back. Keep looking around, but he's not here. I think he's gone.'

'New trauma. Something else has taken his place.'

'I don't know,' said Macleod, 'I don't care. I'm glad to see the back of him. He's the old friend you never wanted.'

'Well, this is the friend you did want, and I'm starving, and we're going to get the Christmas dinner. So come on, lover, let's go.'

Macleod looked over at her. Part of him loved it when she used terms like that. Everyone else was so serious around him. Even when they called him Seoras, it was usually said with a reverence. Jane could tease him. Jane could get under the skin, and he loved it.

He followed her downstairs to the canteen, where several staff assisted them in marching in a long line back up the stairs to the murder squad office. Jane opened the door to a room that was quiet.

'Ho, ho, ho,' she said. 'Merry Christmas.'

Clarissa looked up and laughed.

'Christmas dinner is on the house today,' said Jane, turning and advising some of the staff where to put the plates. A table was moved across and soon Jane stood behind it with two staff, with ladles and passing out party hats. The room took on a fresh air. It wasn't quite uncontrolled festivities, but the team let loose. They settled down with turkey, sprouts, roast potatoes, and thick lashings of gravy. It was followed by Christmas pudding, and Jane stood behind the table with a smile on her face.

'You've enjoyed this,' Macleod said to her.

'I don't get to see your lot enough. I get it. As a team you have to celebrate, but we don't get to be together enough.'

She watched as Angus and Ross's little one entered the room. There was a cry of 'Dad', little feet tearing down, and Ross picking up an excited toddler. Ross smiled at the rest of the team as Clarissa went over to greet him. John arrived shortly after, taking Hope in his arms. Frank arrived with him, and Clarissa embraced him tenderly. Susan was sitting with Patterson, neither of them with partners, talking away to each other, both seeming happy.

Macleod stood up proudly. Then he walked over to John and Hope, indicating he wanted to speak to her.

'I need to take her off your hands,' he said, 'for a moment. It's her time to talk to the team.'

'Why me?' asked Hope. 'It's you.'

'You ran this, you need to end it. Tell them well done. You need to say what's going to happen. Make sure that they understand that this is a win.'

'But that's your job,' said Hope. 'You do that.'

'I did it when I was a Detective Inspector. I did it when it was such a big case that I was running it. You ran this case. This is your speech,' said Macleod. 'Besides, I have other news to say, afterwards. I can't do it all.'

Hope walked up to stand beside Jane and asked her to take a seat. Jane did so and everyone quietened down to look at Hope. She took a step forward in front of the table.

'I've been told that I should do this, that I'm the Detective Inspector,' said Hope. 'More and more, I'll be running the cases. Well, we have Seoras running beside us. Or rather, over the top. I don't know. It's Christmas Day and we're all here. First of all, to us,' said Hope, 'we made it through this alive. Thank God.'

The team raised a glass, 'To us,' said Macleod, and the chorus came, 'To us.'

'Understand this is a win,' said Hope. 'Yes, we lost Tommy Wilson. After the time two victims were already dead and we'd got going on the investigation, we stopped three other people from dying. Three other people that have families to go to, three other people that will eat Christmas dinner. We are here. They're here,' said Hope.

'I am immensely proud of you lot. Seoras always said I should trust the team because he always did. They come up with solutions. I didn't come up with a solution for our Badalisc. That goes to Susan. Our constable kept a mum-to-be and her child alive. I, for one, am so delighted to have her on the team. A lot of you call her mini-Hope. She's not mini-Hope. She's Susan.'

Hope raised her glass and a refrain of 'Susan' was sounded.

Hope saw her colleague smile, and almost blush.

'We wouldn't have a provost without Clarissa. I'd tell you what she did, but we all know.'

'Clarissa' came the refrain, and then Hope looked around her.

'All of you have done incredible work. Ross chased down a carrot'—there were laughs across the room—'and he stopped a Krampus.'

'Ross,' came the shout and loudly. 'Ross' came the refrain.

'This is Christmas,' said Hope, 'and I want to turn to everyone here and look at everyone who's not on this team. Think about those who are maybe still at home. Families, the extended family. They put us here. They keep us here. To everyone else and for me, especially to John, we love you. Thank you. We couldn't do this job without you.'

She focused in on her man and he smiled back. She saw the others looking across at their next of kin, those dear to them.

'We get done today,' said Hope, 'and we'll try to have tomorrow off. You all deserve it.'

'Not to steal her thunder,' said Clarissa, 'but I am going to.' She walked over and gave Frank a kiss and then stood in the middle of the room, looking around her. 'This is it,' she said, a tear in her eye. 'This is really it. It's my last case with you. There will be no more. I'm starting anew and I'm not coming back in, in case you ask.'

She looked at Macleod and laughed.

'I would like to say this has been the most joyous time of my life, but that would be a complete lie. I saw some horrors, some terrible things. Some will stay with me for the rest of my life. Some I am proud to have done, if not enjoyed. I look every day at Patterson knowing I saved his life, and I know it's

218

a life that was worth saving.'

Tears flowed from her eyes.

'I cannot do what you do. Cannot see this death. I cannot put myself in this horror anymore. Even yesterday evening, God help me. Tommy Wilson will live with me for the rest of my life, but I did that to save a man, and I have to remember his face. I have to remember the faces of you who saved me. Only Frank is more grateful than I am for you for that.

'We have backed each other up too many times to mention. I don't look for thanks for what I've done, for you did it for me. We are police officers. This is what we do. We are detectives and we will protect. I will miss working with you, but understand I will not miss this work.'

She turned to Macleod. 'I would give a toast to that man over there for the friend he's been, for the boss he's been, but he's going to remain my boss and I will be remaining in this building. I will no longer be your direct colleague, but I will always remain your colleague and friend. You are always welcome to come and talk to me in my office. It's a bit smaller than some other people's,' she said, glancing at Macleod and then Hope, 'but it'll do me and it will do my new colleague.

'You're not just losing me today, Patterson's joining me. I think he feels the way about this team that I do. Maybe not so emotionally, but he will be a brilliant officer and a tremendous help to me on the arts team. Our squad is not just based here, it goes much more nationwide. We work remote from each other. I can't leave this force at the moment. It's still in me, and Frank knows that. Thankfully, I have married a man who puts me to the fore. By the way, I don't think golf has left his heart either. He'll still be up at that club. It's au revoir, but it is not goodbye.'

The team walked forward embracing her, but she told them to stop and she waved to Patterson, ushering him into the middle of the group. Together, there was an enormous hug and Clarissa cried.

She watched Ross look over at Hope and Hope give a nod, and she saw Macleod smile.

'While we're on big announcements,' said Ross, 'I'll be sitting my sergeant exams. Then, all being well, I'll be the new DS taking over from Clarissa.'

'Good on you, Als,' said Clarissa, tears now flowing completely. She hugged him. For the next five minutes, the team walked amongst each other, hugging and congratulating each other. Eventually, Macleod made his way out of the group to stand with Jane beside the table almost devoid of food. Clarissa walked over to join them.

'Thank you,' she said.

'Thank you,' said Macleod.

'I wasn't talking to you,' said Clarissa. 'I was talking to Jane. She knows I love you to bits, but she's so right for you.'

'There's a Christmas service, a hastily organised one,' said Jane. 'I think there'll be lots of hymns and stuff. Organised in the wake of what happened yesterday. Ordinary people going along. I thought we should go along and be part of a community that needs to heal. It's going to take time.'

'Good idea,' said Clarissa. 'I'm not a church person, but I like the hymns. I can do those.'

Hope came over, and Macleod explained the situation.

'Yes,' she said, 'we should go. This community's been through a rough time. It'll help them to see us there and we should sit together, show we are a team.'

'No,' said Macleod suddenly, 'a family. There's a team here, but there's a family around it.'

He turned and announced to everyone what they were going to do. Ross nodded his affirmation, and Susan and Patterson said they'd join them.

'After all,' said Susan, 'where else am I going?'

Ross's little one ran up towards Macleod, took a running jump, and Macleod fortunately caught him, lifting him up and giving him a cuddle. This was his godson.

'Is Santa going to be at the church?' said the child.

'I don't know,' said Macleod, 'but we're going to be there. Your dads are going to be there, and we're going to sing. I'll teach you how to sing.'

'Make a joyful noise unto the Lord,' said Clarissa suddenly. 'Your godfather can make a joyful noise,' she said to the child. 'But trust me, the one thing it won't be, is in tune.'

They all laughed, and together they walked out of the office, ready to enjoy Christmas together.

The end

Read on to discover the Patrick Smythe series!

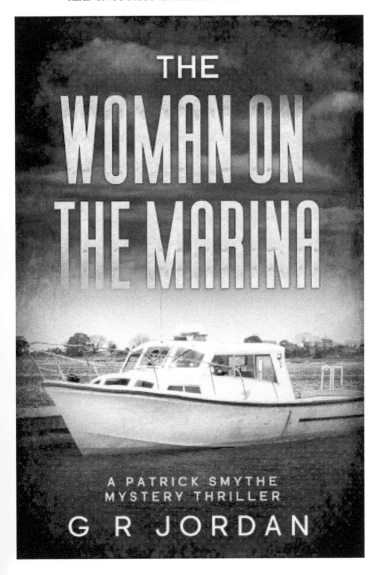

THE
WOMAN ON
THE MARINA

A PATRICK SMYTHE
MYSTERY THRILLER

G R JORDAN

Patrick Smythe is a former Northern Irish policeman who

after suffering an amputation after a bomb blast, takes to the sea between the west coast of Scotland and his homeland to ply his trade as a private investigator. Join Paddy as he tries to work to his own ethics while knowing how to bend the rules he once enforced. Working from his beloved motorboat 'Craigantlet', Paddy decides to rescue a drug mule in this short story from the pen of G R Jordan.

Join G R Jordan's monthly newsletter about forthcoming releases and special writings for his tribe of avid readers and then receive your free Patrick Smythe short story.

Go to https://bit.ly/PatrickSmythe for your Patrick Smythe journey to start!

# About the Author

GR Jordan is a self-published author who finally decided at forty that in order to have an enjoyable lifestyle, his creative beast within would have to be unleashed. His books mirror that conflict in life where acts of decency contend with self-promotion, goodness stares in horror at evil, and kindness blindsides us when we at our worst. Corrupting our world with his parade of wondrous and horrific characters, he highlights everyday tensions with fresh eyes whilst taking his methodical, intelligent mainstays on a roller-coaster ride of dilemmas, all the while suffering the banter of their provocative sidekicks.

A graduate of Loughborough University where he masqueraded as a chemical engineer but ultimately played American football, Gary had worked at changing the shape of cereal flakes and pulled a pallet truck for a living. Watching vegetables freeze at -40'C was another career highlight and he was also one of the Scottish Highlands "blind" air traffic controllers.

These days he has graduated to answering a telephone to people in trouble before telephoning other people to sort it out.

Having flirted with most places in the UK, he is now based in the Isle of Lewis in Scotland where his free time is spent between raising a young family with his wife, writing, figuring out how to work a loom and caring for a small flock of chickens. Luckily, his writing is influenced by his varied work and life experience as the chickens have not been the poetical inspiration he had hoped for!

**You can connect with me on:**

○ https://grjordan.com
f https://facebook.com/carpetlessleprechaun

**Subscribe to my newsletter:**

✉ https://bit.ly/PatrickSmythe

# Also by G R Jordan

G R Jordan writes across multiple genres including crime, dark and action adventure fantasy, feel good fantasy, mystery thriller and horror fantasy. Below is a selection of his work. Whilst all books are available across online stores, signed copies are available at his personal shop.

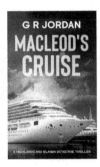

**Macleod's Cruise (Highlands & Islands Detective Book 30)**
https://grjordan.com/product/macleods-cruise
**A recovery cruise turns into a work request. A mystery body leads to consternation for multiple passengers. Can Macleod discover the identity of the victim and unmask the killer before the passenger disembark forever?**

When Seoras Macleod's holiday cruise turns into a work request, he is forced to balance his professionalism with tending to his unamused partner. As he uncovers the secrets the passengers have dragged on board, Macleod finds himself far from home with a killer on his back. Has he still got what it takes when his team are absent? Or will the killer remove the pesky investigator before he cracks the case wide open?

*Relaxation is so often a killer!*

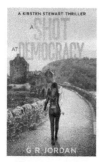

**Kirsten Stewart Thrillers**
https://grjordan.com/product/a-shot-at-democracy
**Join Kirsten Stewart on a shadowy ride through the underbelly of the Highlands of Scotland where among the beauty and splendour of the majestic landscape lies corruption and intrigue to match any city. From murders to extortion, missing children to criminals operating above the law, the Highland former detective must learn a tougher edge to her work as she puts her own life on the line to protect those who cannot defend themselves.**

Having left her beloved murder investigation team far behind, Kirsten has to battle personal tragedy and loss while adapting to a whole new way of executing her duties where your mistakes are your own. As Kirsten comes to terms with working with the new team, she often operates as the groups solo field agent, placing herself in danger and trouble to rescue those caught on the dark side of life. With action packed scenes and tense scenarios of murder and greed, the Kirsten Stewart thrillers will have you turning page after page to see your favourite Scottish lass home!

*There's life after Macleod, but a whole new world of death!*

**Jac's Revenge (A Jack Moonshine Thriller #1)**
https://grjordan.com/product/jacs-revenge

**An unexpected hit makes Debbie a widow. The attention of her man's killer spawns a brutal yet classy alter ego. But how far can you play the game before it takes over your life?**

All her life, Debbie Parlor lived in her man's shadow, knowing his work was never truly honest. She turned her head from news stories and rumours. But when he was disposed of for his smile to placate a rival crime lord, Jac Moonshine was born. And when Debbie is paid compensation for her loss like her car was written off, Jac decides that enough is enough.

*Get on board with this tongue-in-cheek revenge thriller that will make you question how far you would go to avenge a loved one, and how much you would enjoy it!*

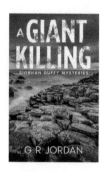

### A Giant Killing (Siobhan Duffy Mysteries #1)

https://grjordan.com/product/a-giant-killing

A body lies on the Giant's boot. Discord, as the master of secrets has been found. Can former spy Siobhan Duffy find the killer before they execute her former colleagues?

When retired operative Siobhan Duffy sees the killing of her former master in the paper, her unease sends her down a path of discovery and fear. Aided by her young housekeeper and scruff of a gardener, Siobhan begins a quest to discover the reason for her spy boss' death and unravels a can of worms today's masters would rather keep closed. But in a world of secrets, the difference between revenge and simple, if brutal, housekeeping becomes the hardest truth to know.

The past is a child who never leaves home!

Milton Keynes UK
Ingram Content Group UK Ltd.
UKHW020849180124
436254UK00001B/21

9 781915 562600